The car filled with tension

And it was all Juliette could do not to unroll her window, just so she could breathe.

"You've changed," Tyler said.

"You haven't."

"You haven't spent ten minutes with me, Jules. How could you possibly know that?"

"It's Juliette."

He laughed and she glared at him hard.

"Okay," he said, "it's Juliette. How'd you know I was back?"

"This is Bonne Terre, Tyler. The second you set foot inside the parish about twenty people called me." As soon as the words were out of her mouth she wished them back. No way did she want Tyler O'Neill to think she'd wasted a single thought on him after he'd walked out on her. No way did he need to think he meant more to her than he did. "I'm the chief here, Tyler. It's my job to know what potentially corrupting influences are hanging around."

Dear Reader,

I was working on *Tyler O'Neill's Redemption* when Paul Newman passed away. I spent days watching movies, reading articles and looking at pictures of this rare and talented man. I was amazed at his charity, his strength of purpose, his commitment to his wife and family. And that's not even talking about his acting or legendary blue eyes. Clearly there will never be another Paul Newman.

But I must admit, all those photos and movies seeped into my brain and onto the page and Tyler O'Neill started taking on some of Newman's real and fictionalized characteristics. Tyler has the eyes and the grin from *Butch Cassidy and the Sundance Kid.* The scorching sideways glances from *Cat on a Hot Tin Roof.* And the devil-may-care attitude and propensity for trouble inspired by *Cool Hand Luke.* How irresistible is that combination?

It's been fun getting Tyler O'Neill out of trouble with the help of Juliette Tremblant—a dangerous woman Tyler loved and left behind. For me, the sparks flew off the page. Please drop me a line at molly@molly-okeefe.com and let me know if they did for you, too. I love to hear from readers.

Happy reading!

Molly O'Keefe

Tyler O'Neill's Redemption
Molly O'Keefe

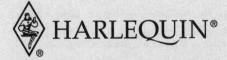

HARLEQUIN®

TORONTO • NEW YORK • LONDON
AMSTERDAM • PARIS • SYDNEY • HAMBURG
STOCKHOLM • ATHENS • TOKYO • MILAN • MADRID
PRAGUE • WARSAW • BUDAPEST • AUCKLAND

Recycling programs
for this product may
not exist in your area.

ISBN-13: 978-0-373-71657-9

TYLER O'NEILL'S REDEMPTION

Copyright © 2010 by Molly Fader.

This edition published by arrangement with Harlequin Books S.A.

For questions and comments about the quality of this book please contact us at Customer_eCare@Harlequin.ca.

® and TM are trademarks of the publisher. Trademarks indicated with ® are registered in the United States Patent and Trademark Office, the Canadian Trade Marks Office and in other countries.

www.eHarlequin.com

Printed in U.S.A.

ABOUT THE AUTHOR

Molly O'Keefe is living out her dream of being a writer, mother and wife. Oddly enough, her dream never seemed to include this much laundry. Or dirty diapers. And, not that she's complaining, but she thought there would be bonbons. Instead there's lots of cold coffee. Nonetheless, life in Toronto, Canada, married to her college sweetheart is wonderful.

Books by Molly O'Keefe

HARLEQUIN SUPERROMANCE

*The Mitchells of Riverview Inn
**The Notorious O'Neills

Don't miss any of our special offers. Write to us at the following address for information on our newest releases.

Harlequin Reader Service
U.S.: 3010 Walden Ave., P.O. Box 1325, Buffalo, NY 14269
Canadian: P.O. Box 609, Fort Erie, Ont. L2A 5X3

For Adam, who understands and helps and listens and takes the kids away for hours at a time.

I love you more every year we're together.

CHAPTER ONE

TYLER O'NEILL WAS WELCOMED back to Bonne Terre the same way he'd been kicked out of it.

With a mouthful of dirt from outside St. Pat's Church.

"I never did like you," Lou Brandt whispered in Tyler's ear while Tyler spit out gravel. "Or your family."

Tyler rolled over and grinned, wincing slightly when his lip split and hot copper blood flooded his mouth. "I've always liked you, Lou," he wheezed. "And your wife."

Lou reared back, his steel-toed work boot poised for another introduction to Tyler's rib cage, but Gaetan Bourdage got a thick arm around Lou's barrel chest. "Come on, now, Lou," he said. Lou strained against Gaetan's arm, his big fat head turning red and purple.

"You're trash," Lou snarled. "You think winning all that money changes things?"

"No, actually," Tyler said, checking to make sure he still had his back teeth. "It just makes me rich trash."

"You're a cheat!" Lou cried.

"Oh, shut up," Tyler moaned. "You're a crappy card player, Lou. You always were and the ten years I've been gone, you've just gotten worse."

Lou strained against Gaetan's arm with renewed fury. "Someone should have shut your mouth for you years ago."

"They tried," Tyler muttered.

"Go on inside," Gaetan said, his Cajun accent thick as

the swamp air. "This boy just ain't worth it." If Tyler didn't know Gaetan, he might just be hurt.

Instead he searched for his cap, finding it trampled in the dust behind him.

"You're right," Lou said, finally easing off. He spit and the thick glob landed in the dirt near Tyler's hand, causing his own temper to flare.

He reared up off the ground, but Gaetan's gaze nailed him to the dirt.

Stay put, his eyes said. *I can only save your sorry ass so many times.*

Lou wandered back to the church and the Sunday night poker game that had been going on in the basement ever since the church had been built, and Tyler hung his pounding head between his knees.

"Welcome home," he muttered.

"Whatchu doing back here, Ty?" Gaetan asked. The old man crouched, his thick silver mustache trembling with anger.

"A guy can't—"

"No," Gaetan said, "if that guy is you, then no. Boy!" Gaetan pulled Tyler up, and even though Tyler towered over the old swamp rat, he was cowed slightly. Coming home had been a bad idea, but coming to the St. Pat's poker game was just stupid.

But then Tyler had a thing for stupid.

"Whatever made you come back, I hope it was worth getting your face beat in." Gaetan pulled a red handkerchief out of his pocket and handed it over. Tyler pressed it to his lip.

Beat in was a stretch, but Tyler wasn't about to get into it with the Cajun.

"I don't know, Gates," Tyler said, instead. "The look

on everyone's face when I walked in there was pretty priceless."

"Priceless?" Gaetan snorted. "Every man in there thinks you cheated."

Tyler bit his tongue and jammed his cap back on his head, trying hard to swallow down the urge that he'd spent the past ten years destroying. Of course, one night back in Bonne Terre and the need to defend himself came crawling back, like a kicked dog.

"I didn't cheat," Tyler said, ready to go back into that church and fight anyone who said otherwise. "Not tonight, not when I was a kid. I never cheated."

"I know that," Gaetan said, scowling, his bushy eyebrows colliding to create a mutant caterpillar. "But you took a lot of their money when you were a boy and they haven't forgotten that."

The satisfaction of taking the money off those men who looked down their noses at his family, called his grandmother names behind her back and watched him out of the corner of their eyes, was still so sweet.

He couldn't help but smile.

Gaetan cuffed him upside the head.

"Hey!"

"You took their money ten years ago and now you come back a rich man to take more?" Gaetan shook his head.

"It's a poker game," Tyler said. "The point is to take each other's money."

"You—" Gaetan curled a hand in Tyler's shirt, pulled him down close to the old man's height until Tyler could smell the whiskey and peppermint on his breath. "You have always taken too much. Always. Even as a boy you could never be happy with what you had. You needed what everyone else had, too. And everyone in this town remembers that about you. You shouldn't have come back here."

It was no big secret. No news flash. He'd been telling himself the same damn thing the whole drive from Vegas to Bonne Terre, but hearing it from Gaetan, a man he'd always considered a friend, stung.

"I know," he said.

"Then why come back?" Gaetan asked. "You're a rich man. A celebrity. You've got that girlfriend—"

Tyler snorted.

"Fine," Gaetan said. "No girlfriend. But why are you back?"

Tyler shrugged. "I have to have a reason?"

"This isn't about your mother snooping around these parts, is it?"

Tyler wished he could tell the old man, but he didn't want to implicate his friend, should it come to that. Instead, he said nothing and Gates sighed.

"You best not drive," Gaetan said, pointing at Tyler's head and Tyler gingerly touched the swelling around his eye.

Lou was a crap card player, but the guy could throw a punch.

Tyler glanced back at his beloved 1972 Porsche, its black paint melting into the shadows. "She'll be okay here?" he asked, and Gaetan snorted.

"Last car stolen in Bonne Terre was the one you stole when you left."

"I doubt that," he said, reluctant to leave Suzy alone and vulnerable outside a place as unwelcoming as St. Pat's.

"Merde, Ty, it's just a car."

"Don't tell that to Suzy."

"Suzy?"

"Suzette, really."

"Lord, Ty, you don't change. I'll watch her myself."

"Thank you. In that case, I might as well take in some

night air," he said, remembering the path through town past the police station and Rousseau Square down to The Manor as if it had been yesterday.

He glanced back in the shadows at his dusty Suzy. He'd get her back in the morning.

"Okay then," Gaetan said. "You come by for dinner or Maude will have your head."

"Will do," Tyler agreed with a grin that split his lip. "Hey, Gates?" The old man stopped, his bowed legs turning him around. "You really mayor?" Tyler asked.

Gaetan nodded. "Sure am, boy, so you best watch yourself."

He winked and walked back into the church, through the lit doorway that led down to the basement. With one last damning look over his shoulder, Gaetan jerked the door shut.

There was a slam and lights out.

Two janitors. The high school wrestling coach. Gaetan and Father Michaels. Suddenly, all too good to play with him.

The reigning World Series of Poker champion.

Which only continued to prove what he'd known down in his gut all along—the world changed but Bonne Terre stayed the same.

Tyler sighed, pushed his A's cap down farther on his head and made his way back home.

The September night was thick and dark, the suffocating blanket he remembered and hated. Two steps and he had that dirty, clammy sweat that made him ache for the white tile shower in his suite, the cool hum of forced air.

Christ, his eye was beginning to pound.

Coming back here had been a dumb idea. He'd been fine, years had gone by without him caring, the memories fading bit by bit, but one word that his mother might be back in town and here he was, choking on the dirt outside St. Pat's.

No doubt the kitchen in The Manor would be empty. None of Margot's sugar pies to welcome him home.

He crossed Jackson and headed for the square, thinking he'd cut through the magnolias in the park and save himself some time, when a dark car slid around the corner, crawling along the curb.

His alley-cat instincts, honed on this very street, woke up and he stepped into the shadows of the trees.

Stupid of him to cross Jackson under the streetlights— anyone looking knew his path home.

The wrought-iron fence was cold against his back. It would be just like Lou to follow him, or call one of his softball buddies to come out here for a little middle-of-the-night batting practice.

The car eased past him, got to the corner and stopped under the streetlamp.

It stopped and waited, exhaust filling the golden pool of light with gray smoke.

Well, crap, Tyler did not like that. At all.

He circled around the other side of the fence, hugging the shadows, between the leaves and the light. If it was Lou's buddies, they wouldn't be expecting him to approach from the side. His foot caught on a branch and he grabbed it from the ground and tested its heft.

Pretty weak, but with some surprise on his side he might do some damage before they took care of what was left of his face.

As he cleared the side of the blue car, blood pumping, smile easing nice and slowly across his face, he saw that there weren't a bunch of men in it. In fact, sitting in the driver's side, staring him right in the eye with ten hard years of hate, was the most beautiful woman he'd ever known.

"Juliette," he breathed. For a second his life stopped and all he saw were those hazel eyes and lips so pink and perfect. And sweet. The sweetest.

"What the hell are you doing here, Tyler?"

JULIETTE WAS NOT, REPEAT, *not* going to touch Tyler O'Neill. Not with her fingers. Not with a ten-foot pole. Perhaps later, when given a chance, she'd touch him good with her fists, but at the moment, there was going to be no touching. Too bad, since it was the only way she was ever going to convince herself the man standing in front of her, as rumpled and bloody and heart-stoppingly handsome as he'd been at seventeen—was real.

And not a figment of all of her furious revenge fantasies.

"Just out for a stroll," he said, tossing the branch he'd been holding onto the dirt.

"Sure you are. What are you doing back in Bonne Terre?" she asked.

"Savannah said The Manor is sitting empty," Tyler said and shrugged, as if his arrival out of the blue after ten years was perfectly natural. "Seems like someone should be watching over it."

"You?" she asked, laughing at the very notion of Tyler being down here for any unselfish reason. "Please."

He stared at her for a second and then smiled.

Her heart fluttered against her chest, a small mechanical bird powered by that smile.

He glanced out at the buildings lining the square, the hardware store and Jillian's Jewelry Shop. The café and the bank. He watched those buildings as if they were watching him back. A threat to be monitored.

"You're right," he said, but that was all he said.

Juliette bit her lip against the other questions screaming to be heard.

Why did you go?

Why didn't you write? Call?

What did I do?

But what would be the point? Ten years of silence were all the answer she really needed.

"Who's been working on your face?" she asked.

"Old friends," he said, touching his eye with careful fingers and wincing anyway.

Something dark and vicious inside of her really liked that he was in pain.

And she hated that she liked it since she'd sworn off feeling anything about this man years ago. But he was here, standing so close she could shoot him, and these feelings—all the old anger and hurt and rage—resurfaced as though they'd just been waiting for the chance.

She'd call him tomorrow, fill him in on what was happening out at The Manor over the phone. Then she'd hang up and never waste another minute thinking about Tyler O'Neill.

She put the car in gear. "Have a good night, Tyler," she said, liking all the cool "go screw yourself" she managed to fit into those words.

"Wait." His hand touched the open window of her car and she pressed her foot back on the brake.

"What?"

"I got an e-mail from Savannah. This guy she's with—"

"Matt?"

"Right, is he—"

Juliette laughed. "You going to stand there and pretend to care, Tyler?"

"She's my sister," he snapped. "Of course I care."

"Then you should show up once in a while."

Tyler's grin was gone and he was looking at her with cold blue eyes that, without a word, damned her straight to hell. Silent, he turned and walked away.

Juliette watched him go, the same long legs, the wide shoulders and narrow hips that looked so damn good in faded and torn blue jeans it made her want to bite something.

Ten years. Ten damn years and he comes back here as if nothing ever happened.

She rested her head against the steering wheel. Maybe nothing had happened. Maybe in the grand scheme of things, a broken heart didn't mean anything. She'd been nineteen, after all, a couple of years of college under her belt, law school at Oklahoma State glimmering in the future—she should have known better than to get tangled with Tyler O'Neill. A high school drop-out who made his living winning Sunday-night poker games and playing piano out at Remy's. He was so opposite from her, he was like a different animal, a force of nature she couldn't ignore. At eighteen he'd been the only thing that could have distracted her from her plan. And he had. He totally derailed her plan.

And now he was back and Savannah was her best friend and things were strange around The Manor these days.

And it was her freaking job to deal with it.

She took her foot off the brake and rolled up next to him.

"Do you want a ride?" she asked, not looking at him. "You've still got another mile to go."

"I know how far it is."

"Then climb in and I'll drive you."

He stopped, sighed, and looked up at the stars as though

he might feel a little of the garbage she felt. After a moment he circled the front of the car, stepping through her headlights, the low beams catching the bright red of his blood on his pale face. Gold-blond hair under his cap and those eyes. Oh, man, those eyes.

And then he was in the car with her and she could smell him, toothpaste and cigars and him. Tyler.

A million memories of hot days and cool nights flooded her. His hands under her skirt, those eyes memorizing every detail of her face, those lips telling her a hundred lies—it all exploded in her head, nearly blinding her.

"Thanks," Tyler said as subdued as she'd heard him. "How have you—"

She cut him off. There would be no "how have you been's?" She knew how he'd been, rich and dating a hot French model whose popularity had them all over every magazine in the grocery store. All month long she couldn't buy a carrot without looking at Tyler holding hands with some stick-thin blonde.

"You should know a few things about what's happening at The Manor," she said, turning left around the square, past the Bonne Terre Inn and toward the road out of town.

"Savannah and Margot are both gone," Tyler said. "And Mom was around a month ago. Savannah told me."

"Not just around," Juliette said, sparing him a glance only to find him watching her. Awareness like icy hot prickles ran down her spine. "She broke into the place twice, maybe three times. She scared the bejesus out of everyone, especially Kate."

"Everyone okay?"

Again she squelched the urge to tell him that if he cared, he should have been there, but she knew it all boiled down in the O'Neill family dynamic with their mother. She'd left scars on her children that could be seen from space.

"Fine," Juliette said. "But Savannah didn't press charges, so Vanessa is out there somewhere."

"Why did she come back?" he asked. "It's been twenty years since she left us here. Why now?"

"She thinks there are gems hidden in the house," she said.

"Gems?" Tyler asked, shaking his head. "The Notorious O'Neills just don't know when to quit. How in the world would gems get hidden in The Manor?"

"Stolen gems from a casino seven years ago. Your mother was involved."

"Of course."

"But so was your dad."

"My dad?" Tyler looked blank for a moment as if the word *dad* had no real connection to him, wasn't even a word he understood. But then there was the shadow. His face changed, and Tyler became harder. Older. As if what his parents had done to him and his brother and sister was a weight he carried, a weight he'd grown used to. Sometimes, though, he got knocked back by how truly heavy it was and how long he'd been carrying it.

Not that she cared. She used to, of course. He'd put on that brooding, grieving, lost-little-boy thing with her ten years ago and her skirts had literally fallen off.

She cleared her throat and stopped at the red light just outside of town. "The house hasn't been broken into again," she said. "But there's been some suspicious activity. Someone's snooping."

"It's still a rite of passage around here to sneak into my grandmother's back courtyard?"

"Not so much," Juliette said. "Not since Matt came along. And what I've found, broken glass, footprints, trampled plants, they're not in the back courtyard. Most of the activity is focused on the sides of the house, the first floor windows into the library."

Tyler's eyes were sharp as knives. "Your father watching my house?" he asked.

She bit back a smile, staring at the white lines on the street. "Dad's not chief anymore, Tyler. But yes, police are watching your house."

"Great," he muttered, his long-standing disdain for local law enforcement, her father in particular, the stuff of legend in Bonne Terre. "So we've got my mother, missing gems and someone trying to break into the house. Anything else I should know about?"

"There's an alarm." She dug into the pocket of her red fitted blazer.

"At The Manor?" he asked. "When I lived there Margot rarely bothered to lock the doors."

"That was a long time ago, Tyler," she said. "Here's the code." She set a piece of paper down on the seat between them. "It's right by the front door and there's another keypad in the kitchen."

"Well," he sighed, picking up the piece of paper and lifting his hips slightly so he could push it into the front pocket of his worn jeans. "Can't say I expected that."

Juliette took a deep breath, wondering whether she should tell him about the other stuff, whether it even mattered to him. She glanced at him, his jaw clenched as he stared out at the darkness around her car.

Was it even her business to tell him?

If not her, then who? No one else was around, and if it could take some heat off his mother, should he see her, then maybe they could all avoid another incident like what happened last month with Savannah.

"Look, Tyler, I don't want to—"

Those blue eyes swung toward her, and she couldn't

deny that as much as she disliked him, she'd never forgotten him.

I thought I knew you, she thought mournfully. *I thought we were friends.*

"Spit it out, Juliette."

"Your grandmother paid your mother to stay away from you kids." Tyler blinked. "Ten thousand a year."

"You know that?"

"Savannah told me. Margot confessed last month when Vanessa broke in again. I'm sorry, Tyler—"

"I've known for years," he said.

"You knew?" she breathed.

He nodded. "How did Savannah take it?"

"Not well," Juliette said. An understatement, but luckily Matt was there to help.

"Carter and I found out and…" He sighed and took off his cap, pushing his fingers through his thick blond hair. "We didn't tell her. We thought…I don't know…we thought we were protecting her. It's all we ever wanted to do."

Juliette took her eyes off the road and gaped at him.

Don't care, she warned herself. *Don't show that you're even interested, because that man will do something awful with the information.*

"Well, I guess that catches you up to speed," she said, pressing on the clutch and shifting into first when the light turned green. She sped up and shifted into second and then as the road opened up she drove it into third.

Tyler's chuckle stirred the hair on her neck. "Juliette Tremblant," he murmured. "You still have a thing for speed." She didn't say anything. Refused to rise to his bait. The car filled with tension until it was all she could do not to unroll her window, just so she could breathe.

"You've changed," he said, and she could feel his eyes on her hair, her body, the clothes she covered it with, and she knew what he wasn't saying—she'd changed, and it wasn't for the better.

"You haven't," she said, not sparing him a glance as she braked over the train tracks.

"You haven't spent ten minutes with me, Jules," he said. "How could you possibly know that?"

"It's Juliette."

He laughed and she glared at him hard.

"Okay," he said, "it's Juliette."

"And you're still the same Tyler O'Neill. Here you are, punched in the face and kicked out of the St. Pat's game. Seems awfully familiar."

"It does ring a bell, doesn't it?" He touched his lip with his finger, probed it with his tongue, and she tried to convince herself it was disgusting. But it wasn't. It was hot.

The air in the car was humid, thick. She cranked the fan a notch higher, hoping it would help.

It didn't.

"Did you know I was back?"

"It's Bonne Terre, Tyler. The second you stepped foot back inside the parish about twenty people called me."

"Good old Bonne Terre," he said, looking around the dimly lit town as though vampires lurked in doorways. Considering she loved this town, and her job was to take care of its citizens, his attitude rubbed her wrong all over. "But what I'm wondering is what you're doing? Keeping up on what's happening at The Manor, giving me a ride." He tilted his head, his Paul Newman eyes practically glowing in the darkness of the car.

Sex oozed off him. And he was breathing all her damn air.

"Your sister is my best friend."

"Right," Tyler said, his voice ripe, his eyes way too warm. "My sister."

She stomped on the brakes. "What are you saying?"

His eyes raked her, that lopsided grin that used to put her whole world on edge was back. "Nothing," he drawled.

His arm stole across the top of the seats, not touching her, but too close anyway.

She leaned over him, ignoring the warmth of his body, the smell of him, all of it. Every memory, every old impulse come back to haunt her—she ignored it all and opened his door.

She'd done what she needed to do. He'd been warned. She could kick him out of her car and, if God was kind, never ever lay eyes on Tyler O'Neill again.

"Get out," she said.

He watched her for a second and suddenly the charm vanished from his smile. All that smug sexuality was banked, put on ice for the moment. "Come on, Juliette—"

"Get the hell out of my car, Tyler."

She met his eyes, unflinching, unblinking, nothing but anger and disgust over his betrayal, his absence, all those years spent ignoring not just her, but Savannah and Margot, too.

"You left without a word," she said, the words burning her mouth, scorching the air. "You are no better than your parents."

Perhaps it was the lights, the shadows, but his face changed. Melted. Just for a moment, as if he couldn't quite keep the mask in place.

But then he eased out of her car into the dark night, taking his scent and his heat and those eyes with him.

"Why did they call you, Juliette?" he asked, slamming the door and leaning in the window. "All the good citizens of Bonne Terre—what made them think of you when I came into town?"

She knew what he thought, that it was their past that had

made people call her. That people saw him and thought of her, that they were linked, forever, in everyone's heads. In her head.

She smiled, so damn happy, thrilled actually, to prove him wrong. "Because it's my job, Tyler."

Slowly, she pushed back her light blazer, revealing her gun.

And her badge.

His jaw dropped and it was beautiful. Really, really a beautiful thing.

"What have you done, Jules?" he breathed.

"It's Chief Tremblant now, Tyler," she said.

Grinning, she popped the clutch and peeled out, emblazoning in her brain this moment—leaving Tyler O'Neill, in a delicious twist, in her dust.

CHAPTER TWO

THE MANOR LOOKED THE SAME.

Shabby but somehow noble. Elegant. A lot like the old lady who lived there, he thought, and suddenly it seemed too long since he'd seen his grandmother.

But just looking at the house, the dark windows, that bright red door, his feet got itchy. His collar tight.

It wasn't home, not for him, and it proved another thing he'd known to be true about himself. If this place, with these women who had loved him with all their hearts, wasn't home—no place was.

He sighed and scrubbed at the back of his neck.

Tired, sore and melancholy, he hoped that if there wasn't sugar pie waiting for him, at least there'd be some of Margot's fine bourbon.

A drink or twelve and some ice on this eye were in order.

But instead of going in the front door, he walked around the side of the house, past the low windows into the library. Trampled grass, broken glass. The window sill had been messed with, but he glanced inside the window and saw small red infrared dots around the room.

Not your average alarm system.

He wondered how a librarian and a retired mistress paying out ten grand in stay-away money a year managed to afford this kind of system.

Must be that Matt guy, he thought. Big shot architect.

A good guy, Juliette had said, but he doubted he could trust her opinion. She used to think Tyler was good, after all.

You're the best, she'd said, her long strong legs wrapped around his, her warm body, sticky with sweat and salt water, wedged between him and the backseat of his old Chevy.

He smiled, remembering how he'd have to peel her off the vinyl while she yelped. He'd felt, that whole summer, as though he was in the middle of a dream. Juliette Tremblant, the sexiest, most untouchable girl he'd ever met, had come home from college a woman. A woman ready to spit in the eye of her police-chief dad. A woman who was tired of the good-girl routine and was ready to see how the other half lived. He'd been more than happy to show her.

Now she was the police chief, just like dear old dad. Man, he did not see that coming. The Juliette he'd known, that feminine creature with the skirts and the lip gloss and the adoring eyes, was so far from the woman sitting in that car with a gun on her hip and a look on her face like she knew how to use it.

What the hell happened? he wondered, walking toward the stone fence that surrounded the back courtyard. He'd thought Jules could become a model, she'd been that beautiful. Her piercing eyes set against that mocha skin she'd inherited from her father had been a lethal combination.

But her heart had been set on law school since she'd been a kid, and he'd assumed she'd become the most beautiful lawyer the state of Louisiana had ever seen.

Not a pseudomasculine police chief.

He sighed and eyed the fence. It was taller, stronger than

it used to be, but Tyler had no problem chinning himself up to the top.

Whoa. The back courtyard, which had been a mess when he'd left, was amazing. Manicured, with a fountain and the trees in the middle and was that a *maze?*

The greenhouse was different and the porch had been extended. Two chairs sat side by side on fresh wooden planks.

A bottle of Jack between them.

The dark bearded man sitting in one of the chairs raised his glass toward Tyler.

"You're late," he said.

Tyler sighed, hanging his aching head for just a moment to wonder why he wasn't surprised before leaping down onto the lush green grass inside the fence.

"Hi, Dad."

JULIETTE PUSHED HER SUNGLASSES up onto her head as she stepped into the station Monday morning.

"Hey, Lisa," she said, walking by the reception and dispatch desk.

"Morning, Jules…ah…Chief."

She and Lisa had gone to school together, and while the Bonne Terre police force didn't operate on formalities, not calling the police chief by her old nickname was one thing Juliette insisted on.

Six months as chief and Lisa was just catching on.

She stepped through the glass doors that led to the squad room and her office. Just like every morning, as soon as she stepped into the common room, all the chatter stopped as if it had been cut off by a knife.

The squeak of her shoes across the linoleum was the only sound in the room until she came to a stop at the night-shift desk, where the men were changing shifts and shooting the shit.

"Morning, guys," she said, taking a sip from her coffee.

"Chief," they chorused. Of the four men sitting there, only two of them managed to say it without the word clogging in their throats. The two she hired from out of town. The other two—Officers Jones and Owens, who had worked with her father and grown up in Bonne Terre— found the word a little sticky.

But she wasn't here to be their friends. She was focused on busting their asses, pushing and shoving them into the twenty-first century, getting them new equipment, and forcing them to change the way things were done in this office.

And she was damn good at her job.

They didn't have to like her, but they sure as hell had to listen to her.

"You've got reports on my desk?" she asked Weber and Kavanaugh, her two new hires who'd pulled the night shift. They nodded and chorused, "Yes, sir."

"Great," she said. "Go on home."

They stood and she stepped into her office, shutting the door behind her. Conversations resumed as she set down her mug and dropped into her chair like a rock.

For some ridiculous reason, she still hadn't redecorated this office. She'd modernized every other part of this force, but not these four walls. And so, it remained exactly the same as when her father had been chief. Dark walls, dress-blues portraits of every police chief Bonne Terre had ever seen, and a big desk upon which she could safely float down the Mississippi.

I should redecorate, she thought. When she'd taken the job she'd been so focused on getting updated computers and fresh blood in the squad room that she hadn't given her office a second thought.

But now, sitting under her father's stern visage reminded her—especially on the heels of a night haunted by thoughts of Tyler O'Neill—of how much Dad had hated Tyler.

There was a word stronger than hated, though. Despised.

Loathed.

Dad had loathed Tyler.

All the O'Neills, to be honest. He'd hated anything, anyone, who rebelled, who embraced disobedience the way the O'Neills did.

Which, of course, had been part of Tyler's appeal. That forbidden fruit thing was no joke.

Dad's attitude toward Tyler had been the same attitude he'd brought to the job, the same attitude he'd rubbed in the face of every juvenile delinquent and small-time crook in Bonne Terre.

His job had been to punish. To control. Dad was a hammer, a blunt instrument wielded without thought to circumstances.

Juliette didn't share his attitude. She thought being police chief was about something else, something kinder.

She wanted to help, not control.

This job isn't for you, he'd told her when she'd applied for the position. *You're too soft. Too willing to forgive when you need to punish.*

She aimed a giant raspberry at her dad's portrait and rolled her chair up to the desk and the small set of reports sitting on her blotter.

A domestic over at the Marones'. Again.

Shirley Stewart escaped from the retirement home. Again. She'd been found on the steps of the Methodist church, unharmed.

Attempted grand theft over at the—

"What?"

She snapped the report open, scanned the perp sheet.

"No, no, no, no," she moaned. She leaped up from her chair and busted into the squad room. "Where is he?" she asked.

"Holding four," Owens said, leaning back in his chair. He jerked his thumb back toward the holding cells as if she didn't know where they were.

"I was supposed to be called if anything happened with this kid," she said.

"What were we supposed to do?" Owens asked, his eyes wide in false and infuriating innocence. "The mayor caught him breaking into the car."

"Where's the car?"

"Impound."

"Do we know whose it is?"

"It's not in the report?" Officer Owens asked. "Your night-shift boys caught it. I can go check it—"

"Do that," she said, so fed up with Owens's laziness and Jones's excuses.

The metal door opened up with a bang under both her hands and she stalked down the small hallway between cells. It was hot and still, the high windows letting in bright bars of sunlight across the gray concrete walls.

Four was back in the corner, and as she got closer she saw him on the floor. His wrists were propped up on his bent knees, the hood of his ragged gray sweatshirt pulled up over his head.

"Miguel?" she said and his head snapped up.

"Chief!" He jerked upright, his legs hitting the cement floor, but his face was still buried in the shadows under his hood. "Chief, I'm so—"

"Sorry?" She asked. "Let me guess, you didn't mean to attempt to steal a—" She glanced down at the report.

"A Porsche," he muttered.

"A Porsche!" She flung her hands up. "I'm trying to help you, Miguel. And you steal a Porsche?"

"I didn't get nowhere. Barely got the door open."

Juliette unlocked the lockbox with the cell keys in it and opened Miguel's cell, the bars slamming back. The sound echoed in the big empty room. "I suppose you were just gonna sit in it?"

"Hell, no," Miguel said. "I was gonna steal it, but Mayor Bourdage found me."

She sat down on the bench next to where Miguel sat on the floor. She was running out of options with this kid, already skirting the line between leniency and not doing her job.

And now he goes and tries to steal a Porsche. It's like he doesn't want my help.

"Miguel, tell me what you think I should do."

His knees came back up and he shrugged. "I don't care."

Maybe her father was right, maybe she was too soft. Maybe this kid, whom she liked, whom she bent every damn rule for, didn't just need a break.

Maybe this kid needed to be punished.

"Look at me, Miguel," she said, biting out the words.

He shook his head and her temper flared. "Stop being so damn predictable." Furious, she reached out and jerked his hood back, revealing his face. The bruises and swelling. The blood.

"My God—" she breathed.

"You think I care what you do to me?" he asked, jerking away, the left side of his face immobile, his eye shut tight from the swelling. He was black and purple from his lips to his hairline, the skin along his cheek seemed to have been burned. She knew things with Miguel's father, Ramon, were bad, but she never dreamed it was this bad. "You think you can do something worse than this?"

"Have you been to the doctor?" she asked.

He sneered and yanked the hood back up.

She leaned back against the brick wall and sighed heavily. Punish him? How? How could she look at what he'd been through and put him in the system? The system would only make him harder. He'd go in there an angry victim and come out a criminal.

It had happened with the last two teenagers she'd sent to the Department of Corrections.

"Where's your father?" she asked.

"Don't know," he said. "Don't care."

"How about you tell me what happened?"

Miguel shook his head. "He was drinking and he went after Louisa." He shrugged, his thin shoulders so small. So young to have to carry so much. "I said something and he picked up this frying pan off the stove."

She winced. That explained the bruises and burns.

"I've got to call community services—"

"I'll tell them I fell down the stairs." Miguel shook his head, emphatic.

"Miguel, you can't be serious. You want to stay with your dad?"

"No, I just don't want to go to no foster home. Louisa and me will get split up and I ain't having that."

"You were going to leave last night, Miguel," she reminded him. "You would have been split up anyway."

"I was going to take her," he said. "I wouldn't ever leave her behind."

Great. Kidnapping on top of grand theft. "I can arrest him, bring him—"

"Yeah, right," he scoffed. "How long this time? Overnight? A week? Last time you did that he came out more pissed off than ever, and me and Louisa had to stay with Patricia."

"But, Miguel, he *hit* you."

"You think this is the first time?"

"Why haven't your teachers reported this?" she asked.

"I skip if it's bad. But it's not usually bad."

"It's my job to report this, Miguel."

"You do what you gotta do, but no social worker is taking me nowhere."

Rock. Hard place. The kid didn't trust the system and frankly, she didn't blame him. Bonne Terre, much less the parish, had no place for a kid like Miguel. It was the streets, holding cell four, or DOC over in Calcasieu Parish. Bonne Terre didn't have a whole lot of crime, but what they did have was largely juvenile-perpetrated and they just weren't equipped to help.

Punish, yes. Help, no.

And this was one of those situations that defined the differences between her and her father. These circumstances dictated that she help this kid.

"We need to get you to the doctor," she said, deciding to put off the question of community services until she had a better answer.

"Am I going to jail?" he asked, and for the first time, something scared colored his voice.

Not if I can help it, she thought.

"Well, it's not up to me. It's up to the guy whose car you tried to steal." He sniffed, the big man, as if it didn't matter, as if jail would be no problem. And maybe, when push came to shove, it was better than home.

But, man, she wanted to give him another option. He

was bright. Smart. Compassionate. He loved his sister, laid down his body for her.

The boy deserved a choice. A chance.

A safe home.

You're soft, her father's voice whispered. *You're way too soft.*

The door to the holding cells opened and Owens walked in, his tall frame casting a long shadow down the hallway. "Got a name on that Porsche," he said, coming to stop in the open door of cell four.

"Yeah?" she asked, her stomach tight. If she could just convince the owner not to press charges, to give the kid a pass, then she'd think of something. A way to give the kid a real opportunity, maybe get him out of that house.

But it all depended on the owner of that Porsche.

"You're not going to believe it."

"Who does the Porsche belong to, Owens?"

"Tyler O'Neill."

CHAPTER THREE

JULIETTE TOOK MIGUEL to the clinic before heading out to Tyler's. She bypassed urgent care altogether and headed straight to the new family doctor who had an office in the clinic.

Dr. Greg Roberts was a good guy. He'd keep his mouth shut, unlike the nurses in the urgent care who lived for cases like this. Bonne Terre was a small town and the most exciting thing the clinic had seen in the past month was when Mrs. Paterson had gotten a little overzealous with her weed whacker and had taken a chunk out of her husband's ankle.

The gossips had turned it into a domestic abuse case before Mr. Paterson's bandages were on.

"Boy said he fell down the stairs," Dr. Roberts said, his voice indicating he didn't believe it for a moment.

"That's what he told me, too." Juliette looked him right in the face and lied, knowing that if she told Dr. Roberts, he'd have no choice but to call in the social workers. Hell, she was supposed to be calling them in herself.

"Chief Tremblant," he whispered, and she knew he was on to her. "What are you doing with this kid?"

His brown eyes were soft and sympathetic and for a moment she was tempted to tell him the jam she was in. They were friends. Sort of. And Greg was smart. Maybe he had an idea, something. Because right now, she had zip.

But Miguel, nearly passed out in the chair outside Greg's

office, shifted and moaned slightly in his doze and Juliette shook her head.

"My job," she told Greg. "I'm doing my job."

"He's what, sixteen? The boy should be in foster care."

"You want to call Office of Community Services? Do it."

"I don't want to fight with you," he said. He stepped closer, the warmth from his body making her slightly claustrophobic. He was a young guy, and occasionally she got the vibe that he was interested. Why she couldn't relax and just go with it was a mystery. "If this kid needs help, I'm on your side."

The man was handsome, and sincere, she had to give him that. But she still wasn't about to let him in.

"I appreciate that, Greg. I do. But I know what I'm doing. There are…circumstances," she whispered.

Greg watched her for a long moment and then held up his hands, indicating he'd back off.

He took a small handful of packaged pills out of his lab coat. "I've given him two. He'll need another two in six hours."

He dumped the samples in her hands, his fingers brushing hers.

Feel something, she willed her nerve endings, *come on, just a little zing.*

But there was nothing.

Of course, because she was an idiot, Tyler O'Neill and his broken-down face and heartless grin popped into her mind, and just the thought of him electrified her, put the hair on her arms on end.

That's what you want? she asked herself ruthlessly. The answer, of course, was no, the by-product of all that fire had been third-degree burns, a life-altering pain.

"Come on, Miguel," she murmured, giving the boy's shoulder a shake. Miguel flinched, then came to, clearly disoriented and drowsy, and she helped him to his feet.

Fifteen minutes later, Juliette stopped in front of The Manor, stared through her window at the red door and took a few deep breaths.

"Hey, Ty," she whispered, practicing her cheerful approach. "You'll never guess, it's funny really, but your car almost got stolen last night."

She pressed her fist to her forehead. "Okay—" she tried straightforward "—look, Ty, we've got a situation. Your car is fine and I need you to work with me. I need you—"

I need you.

Her stomach rolled and her skull pounded. Ten years later and she needed him. Frankly, she'd rather take out her gun and blow off her left toe than face Tyler, but Miguel needed her.

She glanced in the rearview mirror to where Miguel slept, his head pressed to the backseat window, his black hair flat against the glass.

"Please, you son of a bitch," she whispered, "please be reasonable."

FIRE ANTS WERE EATING Tyler's brain and it was making him acutely, painfully unreasonable.

Or maybe it was just his father.

"I'm telling you," Dad said, scrambling eggs without his shirt on. Sunlight coming in through the kitchen window hit his chest hair and put a halo around him.

Ironic. So. Ironic.

"I was staying in Malibu and I grew this beard and everyone thought I was George Clooney. I didn't pay for a meal for three whole weeks."

Tyler listened with half an ear, distracted by the fire ants.

"You listening to me, Tyler?"

"Can't you put on a shirt?" Tyler asked, more concerned about those eggs and his father's copious chest hair.

Richard dropped the spatula. "What is with you? Ty? You didn't say two words to me last night."

"I let you in, didn't I?"

"Yes, and then you slammed the door to your room like a teenager. What happened to your face?"

"It got punched."

"Don't be cute."

"Fine, then you don't pretend that arriving here, of all places, is just business as usual."

Richard crossed his arms over his big chest. Pushing sixty and he still looked good. He could pass for Clooney.

One more scam to add to his repertoire.

"That's what's bothering you?"

"I haven't seen you in eight months! One minute you're living on my couch the next you're gone without a word. I didn't know if you were alive or dead, Dad."

"I told you I was going to L.A.—"

"No, you didn't. You said, 'I miss the ocean.'" Tyler held out his arms in exasperation. "What the hell does that even mean?"

"Okay." Richard nodded, like some kind of grief counselor or something. "I get that you are upset."

Oh, it was hard not to laugh. Dad *got* that he was upset. Hilarious.

"But," Richard continued, "we have things to talk about, son. Things—"

"Gems?" he asked, cutting through the half hour of

bullshit his father was ready to shovel out before getting to the point.

Richard gaped, for just a moment, which was akin to anyone else in the world falling down in a dead faint.

"You know about them?" Richard asked, slowly turning the flame off under the eggs.

"I had a little conversation with local law enforcement last night. Apparently Mom was snooping around here last month looking for some stolen gems. The cop said there'd been some suspicious activity around the house lately. Windowsills damaged, bushes trampled."

Richard pursed his lips. "I've lost my touch."

"Apparently. Why don't you tell me what you know about these gems?" he asked.

"Seven years ago I was hired to steal the Pacific Diamond, Ruby and Emerald from the Ancient Treasures collection at the Bellagio."

Tyler whistled through his teeth and Dad smiled, cock of the walk.

"Right, not easy. Luckily, I had a friend who knew the Bellagio like the back of his hand. He'd been sleeping with one of the pit bosses. Joel Woods—"

"Woods? Why do I know that name?"

"Your sister is traveling the world with Joel's son, Matthew."

Christ. Tyler put his head in his hands and the fire ants went berserk. Could this get any more complicated?

"Where was I during all of this?" Tyler asked. It seemed hard to believe Dad would have been planning a crime of this magnitude while they'd been living together.

"You were shacked up with that dancer," Dad said. "With the legs—"

"Jill. Right." Those had been some heady days. Dad

could have joined the monastery and Tyler probably wouldn't have noticed.

"Who hired you?"

"No idea who the big guy was. I did all my business with a Chinese woman who delivered takeout. They gave me a 60–40 split and bankrolled the supplies."

"How did Mom get involved?"

"That's the thing." Dad spun one of the kitchen chairs around and sat, looking like a wild-eyed sea captain about to tell some tales and Tyler felt that familiar tug-of-war between love and hate.

There was still a part of him that wanted to sit here, listen to every word, applaud every caper and con.

The other part of him was so damn tired of it all.

Ten years ago, Tyler had left Bonne Terre to go find Richard and despite having lived with him off and on for the last ten years, Tyler felt as though he'd never really found him.

Richard Bonavie, nomad, thief, con man extraordinaire, sure. Anybody could follow that guy's trail of broken hearts and cons gone bad across the country.

But Tyler's father? Still missing.

"Seven years ago," Richard said, "when Joel and I got to the drop-off, your mother was there." He shook his head. "I hadn't seen the woman in something like fifteen years and she's sitting in that ratty Henderson bar like she owns the place."

"That must have been a surprise."

"You can imagine. Anyway, I left. If Vanessa was there, I figured the whole thing was sour in a big way."

"What happened to the gems? To Joel?"

"He got pinched, but he only had one gem on him. The emerald. The diamond and ruby are still loose."

"And you think they're here?"

"There was a rumor that the diamond had surfaced in Beijing, but nothing came of it. I think Vanessa picked them off Joel and hid them here. It's why she came back after all these years."

Twenty, to be exact, and Dad was probably right—she sure as hell didn't come back for her kids. Just like Dad, it would take something shiny and very, very valuable to get her coming around.

"So," he said, "you're here for the gems?"

"Of course!" Richard cried, spreading his arms. "There's a fortune hidden in this house, Ty. A fortune that could be ours."

A fortune.

Of course.

"I would think a fortune in gems might warrant some enthusiasm," Richard said, arching an eyebrow.

Luckily, a pounding at the door saved Tyler from having to answer and he stood.

"I'm not here," Dad said and Tyler shot him a look.

"You never are," he muttered and headed to the front door, ready to take off the head of whatever salesperson or Jehovah's Witness might be unfortunate enough to be standing there.

Not bothering with a shirt he swung open the bright red door only to find Juliette Tremblant standing there, straight and tall, her hazel eyes set into that perfect face.

His stomach dipped, his skin tightened at just the sight of her. Her perfume, something clean and minty, hit him on a breeze and his poor, battered body responded with a growl.

"Chief Tremblant," he said, propping his arm up on the door frame.

Oh, the fire ants sat up and cheered when she watched

his chest, her eyes practically sticking to his arms. His hands.

Well, looky, looky, he thought, glad he hadn't bothered with a shirt yet.

"Something I can do for you?" he asked, hooking a thumb in the low waist of his jeans.

Juliette sighed, looking up at the sky as if praying for strength.

"Once again, Jules, I say spit it out."

"Someone tried to steal your car last night."

Fire. Ants.

"Suzy?"

"Who?"

"My car. Where is it?"

"You named your car?"

"Where is my car?"

"It's fine." She put out her hands, and even though she was inches from contact he could feel the heat of her fingers against the bare skin of his chest. Like ghosts. Like memories.

For a second his head spun.

"Your car is fine," she repeated, and he snapped back into clarity. "It's in impound down at the station."

"And who tried to steal it?" he asked, ready, seriously ready to take out every ounce of anger he had about his father and Juliette and being back in this backwater town on the car thief.

Juliette turned and pointed to the sedan in front of the house. A person's head was pressed against the glass of the backseat window, where he'd clearly passed out.

"He did," she said.

"A drunk?" he asked. Just the thought of what could have happened to Suzy at the hands of a drunk made him nauseous.

"A kid," she said. "He's just a kid."

"A drunk kid?"

His stomach was never going to be the same.

"No," she said. "You've got it wrong. Come on, Tyler, get dressed and I'll explain it on the way to the station."

Tyler watched her, sensing something else at work. Her aggression was banked, and she wasn't just being civil. No, she was apprehensive. And mad about it. And the longer he stared at her, the worse it got, until finally her hazel eyes were shooting out sparks.

"Please," she said through clenched teeth and Tyler smiled.

A supplicant Juliette. The fire ants went home and his day just got a whole lot better.

"Well." He grinned and he could hear her grinding her teeth. "Since you asked so nice, Chief Tremblant, I would be delighted to head on down to the station to get my car and press charges against the juvenile delinquent who had the balls to try and steal Suzy."

"Fine," she snapped. "Get dressed."

Tyler ducked back inside to grab a shirt.

"Who's the girl?" Dad asked, standing at the living room window, lifting the curtains an inch so he could stare at the porch.

"No one," Tyler said, grabbing his shirt from the counter where he'd thrown it last night. It stank of blood and dirt and smoke and there was no way he was putting it back on and getting in a car with Juliette Tremblant. Bad enough his face looked like hamburger.

But all of his clothes were in Suzy.

"Give me a shirt," he said, stepping into the living room.

Dad pointed to his open duffel on the couch, still look-ing through the window. "She looks like police."

"She is," Tyler said, slinging through Dad's shirts. There were a bunch of them, which made Tyler nervous about his father's travel plans. Or lack thereof. "Do you even play golf?" he asked, finally picking a gray shirt from the golf-themed collection.

"What are police doing here?" Dad asked, tight-faced and still.

"Calm down," Tyler said. "It's got nothing to do with you."

Dad cocked his head and pursed his lips, his eyes getting a little too speculative. "I'd almost say too bad. Shame for a woman like that to be wasted on a badge."

Something red and boiling bubbled through him, making his hands twitch. His eye pound.

"Well, don't worry about it. I'll handle her."

Dad whistled low through his teeth and Tyler wanted to put his fist through something.

"Later," Tyler said, shoving his feet into his worn down boots. "Try and stay out of trouble."

"No guarantees, son," Dad said, a big grin across his face. "No guarantees."

"So," Tyler said as they approached the sedan and the passed-out would-be car thief in the backseat. "How much trouble will this kid be in?"

Juliette stopped at the curb. "You didn't have any luggage last night. Where'd you get that shirt?"

Crap. Didn't think that through. Chief Tremblant was no dummy, clearly.

Tyler shrugged. "It was in The Manor," he said, pushing at the too-big gray golf shirt. "That Matt guy must have left it."

Juliette nodded, her jaw tight under the aviator sunglasses she wore. "You see anything strange around the house?"

"Strange?" Tyler asked, painfully aware that he was lying to police already, much less Juliette.

I'm back in town less than a day, he thought, bitter and tired. *And I'm already down this road with her.*

Thanks, Dad.

"Broken windows?" Juliette asked. "Any sign of entry at all?"

Nothing except a sixty-year-old thief looking for a fortune in gems.

He shook his head. "Nothing as far as I could see," he lied, the words uncommonly thick in his mouth. Part of being a Notorious O'Neill was the ability to lie like it was poetry, and he'd forgotten Juliette's effect on that particular family trait. She made him sound as practiced as a choir boy lying to the Holy Father.

Something about her eyes, the way she looked at him as if she expected the worst but hoped for better—it was like static electricity. It made him want, so badly, to be a different man. And so the lies—they just curled up and quivered in his mouth.

Complicated. Complicated. Complicated.

"So," he said, easing into the passenger seat, turning to look in the backseat. "About the kid—"

Bright sunlight splashed across the mess that was the boy's face. Burns. Bruises. Stitches at his lip and eye. Somebody had gone to town on the boy, with fury. Hate, even.

Made his stomach turn just looking at it.

Juliette started the car, the sound of the engine ripping through his head.

"What happened to him?" Tyler asked through a dry throat. He turned back around to stare out the windshield at the trees and sunlight, birds and foxes at the side of the road, everything normal and right in the world.

But the boy's face stuck in Tyler's head.

Juliette glanced at him, her hands white-knuckled on the steering wheel. "His father," she said.

"Did that?"

Juliette nodded and he swore. Something dark and slimy twisted in his stomach. Richard was no prize, and frankly neither was his mother—but to do that? To a kid?

"He tried to steal your car to get away. He was going to pick up his ten-year-old sister and leave town."

"In a 1972 Porsche? The clutch is pretty tricky. I doubt the kid would have been able to get it out of the parking lot."

"I'm guessing he wasn't thinking too clearly," she said, her voice that sweet sad drawl he remembered and it curled through him like smoke. Made him want to touch her, feel her skin.

Lord, this whole situation sucked. His car. This tragic beat-up kid in the back. Juliette. It was enough to bring the fire ants back.

No way he could send that kid off to jail.

"Tyler, I need you—" she said, and that voice and those words were a sledgehammer against his head. His whole body shook. "I need you to not press charges. Just pick up your car. Let this go."

"Let this go?" he asked, incredulous. He wasn't going to send the kid off to jail, but he didn't think the boy should go running off to freedom quite so easily, either. "Juliette, I'm not one for letting things go—"

"Really?" she asked. "Could have fooled me."

He wasn't about to get into this right now. Not with this kid's beat-up face stuck in his head and Suzy having been violated outside a church of all places.

"Tell me," he said, leaning back against the passenger door, watching her. "What's going to happen if I let it go?"

"The real question is what will happen if you don't." She pushed her sunglasses on top of her head, displacing her long black hair. Shorter than it had been, but still so bright and so dark it reflected blue in places. "DOC," she said. "I'm just trying to keep him out of jail. You remember how that felt."

Her level gaze sawed him in half, cut through all that bullshit he carried and laid him to waste. Reminding him, in a fractured heartbeat, of every noble and kind thing she'd ever done for him, and how he'd never done a single thing to deserve it.

"Juliette," he breathed, regret a suffocating pain in his chest.

She shook her head. "This isn't about us, Tyler. It's about the kid. It's about giving Miguel a chance."

CHAPTER FOUR

JULIETTE HELD HER BREATH, waiting, praying that the guy she hoped existed, buried deep under Tyler's selfish, childish nature, would speak up and tell her he wasn't going to press charges.

It seemed like such a long shot.

Suddenly she was struck by a gut-wrenching fear that keeping Miguel out of the system wasn't the right thing to do. Too many people knew what she was doing now—Dr. Roberts, who was putting himself and his career on the line for a kid he didn't know and a woman who held him at arm's length, and Tyler, who'd proven to be about as trustworthy as a toddler on a sugar high.

Maybe she needed to reassess this situation, but how? What other alternatives were there, for her or for Miguel? Juliette pulled in front of the gates at the impound yard behind the station and faced Tyler.

"So much for defending Suzy's honor," Tyler said and Juliette nearly collapsed with relief. "I won't press charges, but what happens now?"

"Well, you get your car and go about your business."

"What happens to the kid?" Tyler asked. "Some kind of public service? A community thing? Picking up trash on the highway?"

Juliette shook her head. "I…I don't know yet."

"Don't know yet?" Tyler asked. "Aren't you chief?"

"We don't have any kind of program—"

"So he steals my car and you just let him go?" Tyler asked.

"Of course not, Tyler. I'm not saying he won't be punished in some way, I just haven't figured it out. But I will."

"You could always ask your father," Tyler said, something in his voice ugly and mean. "He had some creative ways for dealing with kids who broke the law."

He was right. And frankly, he was right to be mad. But ten years after Tyler had left her without word or warning, she wasn't about to apologize for her father's mistakes.

"That wasn't about the law," Juliette said through her teeth.

"I know," Tyler said. "Your father made it real clear why he and his goon were kicking the crap out of me."

She felt him watching her, but she didn't turn, didn't engage in this fight with him. The past—their past—was dead and buried.

"You've gotten cold, Jules," he said. "A few years ago you'd have torn my head off."

She wanted to snap at him, to turn her head and scream every foul and hateful thing she'd ever thought about him. She wanted to punch him and scratch his face—hurt him like he hurt her.

But what would be the point?

"You have no idea, Tyler," she said instead, wrapping herself around her icy-cold hate for Tyler O'Neill and the meager victory she'd won for Miguel.

TYLER SIGNED THE LAST of the papers and followed Juliette out into the impound yard. It broke his heart to see poor Suzy surrounded by junkers with wreaths of parking tickets under their wipers.

She deserved so much better.

He watched Juliette, the sun turning her hair to ebony. Her body, so tall and strong. Her grace had become something disciplined. Something controlled. Powerful.

It was making him nuts. It was why he'd tried to provoke her in the car, watching her hands on the wheel, her eyes on the road. Queen of her kingdom.

He wanted to knock her down a few pegs, remind her of that totally different girl he'd left behind.

But not you. Some awful, righteous, pain-in-the-butt voice inside his head asked, *You're still the same, aren't you?*

"Here you go," she said, unlocking the gate, swinging the chain link back. She stood back, her hand on her thin waist, her black pants tight across her thighs. Her hips.

He swallowed, tossing his keys in his palm. Trying to be casual. Pretending that something wasn't shaken inside of him.

When he'd made the stupid decision to come back to Bonne Terre it had never occurred to him that Juliette would still be here. If he'd have thought he'd run into her, he never would have come. Because it hurt to look at her, it hurt to be reminded of what he'd felt that summer—of who, for three short months, he'd let himself believe he could be.

"Thank you," Juliette said, brushing off her hands, "for being cool about—"

He put his hand up, shaking his head. The years behind them, the way he'd left, those nights in the bayou, what she'd done for him in the end.

"It's the least I could do, Juliette."

For a second her face softened, and she was the girl he'd known. The girl who had made his head spin and his heart thunder with stupid dreams, a million of them put right into her soft hands.

"It's a good thing you're trying to do," he said. "With that boy."

She opened her mouth as if to say something, but in the end thought better of it and just nodded.

He slid his key into the lock of Suzy's door, every instinct fighting against the stupid impulse he had to touch her. Just once more. For all the years ahead.

Do not, he told himself, trying to be firm, trying to be reasonable, *get yourself worked up over this woman again. Don't do it.*

"You know," he said, turning to face her again, the sun behind her making him squint, his eye pound. "Your dad was right."

"About what?" she asked on a tired little laugh that nearly broke his heart.

Don't do it, you idiot.

Her eyes snapped, the air around them crackled. The impulse, the need to touch her was a thousand-pound weight he could not ignore or shake off.

She will take off your head and feed it to a dog, man. Do not be stupid.

But in the end he ignored the voice because she was a magnet to everything in him searching for a direction. He stepped close, close enough to breathe the breath she exhaled. Close enough to smell her skin, warm and spicy in the sunlight.

Her eyes dilated, her lips parted, but she didn't move, didn't back away and his body got hot, tight with a furious want.

The air was still between them, as if they were frozen

in time. But inside he raged with hunger for her. Always for her.

He lifted his hand, slow, careful, ready for her to snap but she didn't. He placed his calloused, shaking fingers against the perfection of her cheek. Her breath hitched and for a moment—the most perfect moment in ten miserable years—Juliette let him touch her.

And then, like the good girl she was, she stepped away from the riffraff. Her eyes angry, her skin flushed.

"You're way too good for the likes of me, Juliette Tremblant," he murmured.

He got in Suzy and slammed the door. The humidity inside the car was an insulation between him and her, an insulation he needed. He needed metal and barbed wire and pit bulls straining at their leashes between them, because he knew, like he'd always known—underneath her totally justified anger, her reluctance, her disgust—he knew Juliette Tremblant wanted him as much as he wanted her.

I can't see her again, he thought, starting the car, Suzy's rumble a welcome sound. Familiar. This was his world. Suzy, his father waiting at home, the clothes on his back, his money in the bank.

And there was no place in it for Juliette.

And there was no place for him in Bonne Terre.

He was an O'Neill. One of the most notorious of them all, which meant that Juliette and the past and those fledgling dreams he thought he'd forgotten about were wasted on him.

And whatever he thought he was going to find in Bonne Terre, whatever peace or solace he was looking for—it wasn't here. It wasn't anywhere. Not for him.

Gaetan was right—he was always wanting what other people had. Coming back to The Manor, looking for the kid he'd been, the family he'd known. That wasn't for him.

He got hotel rooms and card games. One-night stands with women so beautiful they could only be fake. Late nights and later mornings, days vanishing under neon signs. That was his life. That's what he got.

And it was time to get back to it.

JULIETTE SHOOK. FROM the inside, through her blood and muscles, from her hair to her fingers, she shook with anger.

Oh, and don't forget the lust. The lust that churned through her and over her and under her.

She slammed the impound door too hard and the chain link rattled and bounced back at her. So, she slammed it again. And again. Her hair flying, the gate rattling and crashing.

"Damn him!" she screamed, slamming the gate so hard it bounced, rebounded and stuck shut.

Damn him.

Ten years without a word, after what she'd done for him. After what she'd given him in the cramped backseat of that stupid Chevy he used to drive. Ten years. And he waltzes back here and realigns everything.

She put her hands on her hips, feeling the weight of her badge and gun, the solid strength of those things against her hips. She was not the girl she'd been, and Tyler O'Neill was not going to ruin her life again.

"Chief?"

She turned and found Miguel standing beside the back door of her sedan.

Great, she thought, *just what I need. Miguel with an earful.*

"You okay?" Miguel asked, his concern fierce and palpable. She melted a little; her little hoodlum was so gallant.

"I'm fine," she said, and took a deep breath. "And, actually, so are you. The owner of the Porsche isn't going to press charges."

"Tyler O'Neill?" Miguel asked.

"How do you know that?"

"I recognized him in the car. I've seen him playing poker on TV. He's rich, huh?"

"Hard to say," she said. "Not much ever sticks to Tyler." She turned back to Miguel, narrowing her eyes. "You were just pretending to sleep in the backseat, weren't you?"

He nodded, unapologetic. Probably a skill he'd learned to survive.

"I'm not going to jail?" Miguel asked, as if he couldn't believe it. Juliette put her hands on his shoulders and waited until he looked at her. The impact of his wounds could still take her breath away and she wondered again whether she really was doing the right thing, or if calling in the social workers wasn't the way to try and save this boy.

"It's not too late," she told him. "I can call the Office of Community Services—"

Miguel shook his head. "I'll run. I swear it."

He wasn't lying. And while she didn't doubt that she'd be able to find him, if he took his sister, who knew what kind of trouble might find them before she did. Two kids, no money—it was a disaster in the making.

"Okay," she said. "But we've got to keep you away from your dad. Where is he now?"

"It's Monday, so he's sleeping it off and then he's back out at the refinery until Saturday." The refinery was over the state line, and employed many of the men and women of Bonne Terre. Due to the commute, many of them, like Miguel's father, spent part of the week in a cheap hotel closer to the refinery.

"Your sister?"

"She's at Patricia's. I'm gonna pick her up for school tomorrow." Patricia was an old friend of Miguel's mother, who did what she could for the kids, but the woman was eighty, on welfare and barely spoke English.

She nodded. What to do? What to do?

"All right." She ducked her head, looking hard into his good eye. "Tomorrow after school you come right here. In fact, after school you come here every day."

"To the *police station?*" he asked, horrified as any good delinquent would be.

"It's your only choice, Miguel. And considering what I've done for you, if you don't show up I'll be—" He looked away. "Miguel," she snapped and he looked back up, sighing. "I will be very, very insulted."

Miguel nodded, his lip lifting slightly. Nearly made her cry to see it. Here he was, face beat in, future up in the air, and the kid could still smile. Sort of.

Maybe she could make this work—as long as Dr. Roberts didn't tell anyone and Tyler kept his mouth shut. And if no one in the station cared about an attempted grand theft she made disappear, or wondered why Miguel was cleaning squad cars every day after school.

And particularly if no one else saw Miguel's file.

Panic nearly swamped her. Who was she kidding?

Thinking about what she was doing made things worse. She needed to move, act, do something. Give Ramon Pastor a warning that even he would understand.

"Get in the car," she said, following Miguel toward her sedan.

"Chief!" Lisa came running out into the impound yard, her blond ponytail a little flag out behind her.

"What's up?" Juliette asked, a little surprised to see Lisa away from her FreeCell game.

"Mayor wants to see you," Lisa said.

It had been approved? She'd just turned in that paper-work last week. The squad car requisition? Man, the mayor was totally on her side—

Lisa's eyes flipped over to Miguel. "About the boy."

"DAD!" TYLER CALLED, slamming the front door shut behind him.

"Yeah?" Richard stepped in from the kitchen into the hallway, a sauce-splattered apron tied around his trim waist. Good God, the man was playing house.

"Let's go," Tyler said to Richard's blank face. "Let's go back to Vegas. Play some cards, get a steak as big as our heads."

"I'm making lasagna."

"Screw the lasagna!" Tyler cried. "It's time to go."

"But we just got here. We haven't found the gems."

"Dad, if it's about money, I've got more than—"

Richard shook his head. "I'm not taking your money."

Tyler blew out a long breath and stared up at the ceiling. This totally misplaced sense of honor his father had could be such a pain in the butt. "You will live in my suite, charge meals to my room and wear my damn clothes, but you can't take money from me?"

"Hey—" Richard wiped his hands off on the apron "—that's taking care of one another. You'll remember I did the same thing for you for years after you found me in Vegas."

I was a kid! Tyler wanted to yell. *I was your kid! It's part of a father's job description.*

But the truth was, Richard often got the job description for father and sperm donor confused.

I should just leave. Leave him here to find these non-existent gems. Tyler's feet twitched with the urge to turn around and walk away, leave Richard behind like he'd done to his family. Shuck them all like so many dirty socks.

If he could leave the best of them behind, why the hell couldn't he walk away from the worst of them?

"I need you, son," Richard said, his voice getting earnest, his eyes slightly damp. The old caring father routine—*I may have been absent, but you were never absent from my thoughts.* Tyler fell for that story hook, line and sinker more times than he'd like to admit.

"You need me to help you look for gems," Tyler said, crossing his arms over his chest. "You could hire someone for that. Hell, we could get a cleaning crew in here and they'd—"

There was something off on Dad's face, something raw. Something not manufactured and it looked like worry.

"What?" Tyler asked, feeling his stomach fall into his shoes.

"It's not a big deal—"

"What aren't you telling me?"

"I was in a…thing…back in Los Angeles."

"Oh, my God," Tyler breathed, turning away from his father, fisting his hands in his hair. "Oh. My. God."

"I didn't do anything," Richard said. Tyler heard him step forward and Tyler put up his hand. If the old man got closer there was a good chance Tyler would knock him out. "I swear to you, son, I didn't do anything. But the friend I was staying with was arrested for credit-card fraud. I didn't know what he was doing, but because—"

"But because you were staying with him, the police think you do." Tyler sighed and looked his father hard in the eye, willing his father to tell the truth.

"I was questioned and released. I swear, son," he said. "I had nothing to do with it. Credit-card fraud is for lowlifes."

Tyler's laughter was a hard bark that hurt his throat. "Good to know you have standards."

"I just need…a change of scene, until things cool down. Just for a little while."

"What if I decide to leave?"

"Then I'd wish you well," he said, "but I better stay. Empty house and all."

Empty house full of gems.

"It's not your house."

"Not yours, either."

Son. Of. A. Bitch.

There was no way Tyler could leave now. It would be like walking away from a bomb with a lit fuse. There was simply no telling what kind of trouble Richard would get into unattended. And if he wasn't here, Juliette would drive by, checking on The Manor. It was only a matter of time before she found Richard.

"I need a drink," he muttered.

"WHAT WE NEED IS A PLAN," Richard said an hour later, pouring another finger of whiskey in the old crystal tumblers. Tyler picked his up, loving the paper-thin edge of the glass against his lips and the solid heft and weight in his hands. Made him want to bite it and hurl it against a wall.

Sort of how he felt about his father.

About Juliette. Lord, how was he going to be able to avoid her now? In a town this size? Impossible.

"What we need is to stop drinking, start looking," Tyler said, drinking anyway.

"I've been looking," Richard said, stretching back in his chair, crossing his legs at the ankles.

They sat on the back porch, the early afternoon sunlight a bright warm blanket across their legs, the whiskey a warm blanket in his stomach. Thoughts of Juliette like a sore tooth he just could not leave alone.

More whiskey would fix that, he thought, taking a half inch from the glass. Which was why he was drinking instead of looking, because first things, after all, were first.

Gotta get Juliette out of my head.

"Yeah? Where have you been looking?"

"I started in the basement," Richard said, looking out over the maze and the greenhouse. "Boxes of paperwork. I tell you—" he smiled, shaking his head "—that little girl of mine is a packrat—"

Tyler stiffened, his skin suddenly too tight. Bright sparks in his head. *Don't call her that,* he wanted to yell. *You don't get to call her that.*

But he bit back the words.

"Margot still raising orchids?" he asked, unable to look directly at his father without the help of much more booze.

"I wouldn't know, son. Margot and I never discussed hobbies."

Tyler stood and stepped onto the lush green grass, a miracle in the end-of-summer heat, and crossed the yard, his fingers touching the silvery green leaves of the trees. Soft. But not soft like Juliette.

"Hey, why the sudden interest in finding the gems, Ty?" Dad asked, following him across the grass. He stumbled a little, but righted himself with grace. Dad never could hold his liquor, but he was about the most gracious drunk Tyler had ever seen. Whiskey turned the old man into royalty. "This morning you could care less."

"We've got nothing else to do," Tyler said.

"You don't believe me about the gems, do you?"

"I don't believe one way or the other," Tyler answered.

And he didn't. He didn't actually care, either. At this point he was babysitter/bomb squad, and if the baby wanted to look for gems—what did it hurt?

"You aren't excited about the money?" Dad asked.

Tyler shook his head. He had more money than he could spend in five years, and considering the way money rolled out of his hands, that was saying something.

But with this last win, he'd finally taken his brother, Carter's, advice and talked to a money guy. Tyler got a nice little check every month from his investments.

Carter, he thought, the whiskey making him fond rather than irritated at the thought of his brother. Leave it to the Golden Boy to find a way to run a con on nothing.

Tyler stepped into the greenhouse, which was warm and humid, like breathing underwater. Plants lined a table, and more hung from baskets. No blooms, just the young shoots, green arrows out of dark soil.

Margot was starting over with her orchids and he had to wonder why. He took a sip and touched the soil in one of the baskets. Dry, but not very, considering Margot was on some cruise and Savannah was off falling in love in Paris.

Someone was watering the plants, and it could only be Juliette. Always Juliette.

He found the hose coiled in the corner and turned it on, finding the balance between a trickle and a flood, just like Margot taught him a million years ago.

"Orchids are particular," she'd said, filling the hanging pan under a pink flower. "Some want water from the bottom, some want it from the top. Some want lots, some barely any."

"Seems like a lot of work," he'd said, pissed off at the world because he knew why he was here and that his mother was never coming back. He didn't want to take

care of the damn plants, he wanted to smash them. Break those little pink flowers into pieces.

"That's why I need your help," she'd said, looking right at him, right down to that twitchy dark place. She knew he wanted to wreck her flowers. Wreck everything. And still she wanted his help.

"I don't know what to do," he said, scowling.

"I'll show you," she said, putting the hose in his hand.

"You think the gems are in here?" Richard asked, digging into one of the pots, crushing the green bud with his big, fat, clumsy fingers.

"No, Dad," he said, and flicked the hose at him as if Richard was a cat digging in a house plant.

"Hey! Watch it!" Richard said, bouncing away, bumping into a worktable.

"I don't think the gems are here," he said. Splashing a little water in each of the pots, he didn't know which was which. Which, if any, needed special care.

He turned off the hose, flinging it back in its corner. The last sip of whiskey burned a familiar trail down his throat. An odd longing bobbed in his chest, an unvoiced wish for something he didn't even understand.

I miss this place, he thought. *I miss Margot and Savannah. I miss Juliette.*

He thought of who he'd been, that boy with those bright green dreams pushing out of the rotten soil his mother had planted him in.

The thought, as soon as it was fully formed and poisonous, was plucked out. Destroyed.

Wishing for something different was a waste. These were the cards he'd been dealt, and if he didn't like them—too bad.

He was Tyler O'Neill, born a card man, from a long line of con men and petty crooks. This was his life.

And the best thing he could do for Juliette Tremblant was to keep himself and Dad far away from her.

He tested the weight of the tumbler in his hand. Tossing it. Catching it. Fine crystal, it was so perfect. Better than a baseball.

The tumbler rocketed through the air—a perfect arc, catching the light at its zenith, splashing rainbows across the courtyard—and then smashed against the stone wall, fracturing into a million glittering pieces.

"Tyler?" Dad asked, his voice careful.

"I'll start in the upstairs bedrooms," he said, and headed back to the house.

CHAPTER FIVE

"WHERE'S THE BOY NOW?" Mayor Bourdage asked, sitting behind the giant desk in his office.

"I dropped him off at home," she said.

The mayor tore open a packet of Alka-Seltzer and dumped it into the glass at his elbow, the water exploding into bubbles. The man looked decidedly gray.

So, she imagined, did Father Michaels, the wrestling coach and Lou Brandt.

The good old boys really tied one on during those Sunday-night poker games.

The mayor drained the glass in three large gulps and then wiped his face. "The kid looked like he'd gotten into it with a freight train."

"His father, sir."

"His father did that?"

Juliette nodded.

"Merde," Mayor Bourdage whispered. He set his empty glass down on a coaster, taking a long moment to push the glass and coaster across his giant desk.

"If you don't mind me asking, Mayor, do you just want an update or was there something you needed from me?"

"What are you going to do with that boy?" he asked.

As Gaetan leaned back in his chair, sunlight fell across his face and he winced. Swearing, he rolled his chair out of the sun's direct path.

His concern for Miguel might just be the help she needed, but she had to be sure of the mayor's sympathies first.

"Why are you asking, sir? It's not city-hall business."

"I found the kid trying to steal that car, Juliette. That makes it my business. And this isn't the first time he's been brought in."

Gaetan slipped on a pair of reading glasses and opened a file on his desk, and Juliette recognized Miguel's sheet. *How in the world did he get that?* Juliette thought, standing speechless and stupid.

"He was brought in a few weeks ago for getting in a fistfight with his father? At the…" He scanned the page, lifting a sheet.

"The grocery store." *Owens,* she thought, a tidal wave of anger sweeping through her. This was the last straw. The man needed to be reminded who was boss and damn if she didn't look forward to reminding him.

"Witnesses say your boy attacked his father. And yet you let him go."

This was it. Her reckoning for making the wrong call with Miguel.

"We brought him and his father in, they both cooled off, and we let them both go. Miguel has never been charged with anything. Or convicted. He's a boy with absolutely no guidance. His father is an abusive drunk, his mother is gone. He's trying to keep his sister safe."

"By attempting to steal a car?"

Juliette sighed. "I know what it looks like, but if we send him to DOC you know what will happen."

"I do indeed." Mayor Bourdage nodded. "But you're walking a very thin line here, Chief. So, I ask again, what are you going to do?"

"I'm working on it," she said, unsure of what she could

do with Miguel. "I thought maybe he could clean some cars after school."

Mayor Bourdage's eyebrows hit his hairline. "Boy tried to steal a car and you're making him clean squad units?"

"It's a beginning," she said, feeling her ears burn. "But we have no community service arrangements, no programs for at-risk kids, no counseling for families—"

"We're a town of two thousand people. The parish handles all that. Foster homes and—"

"We need something here, in Bonne Terre. Our juvenile-perpetrated crime is up almost a hundred percent over the last two years."

"Which is a good reason not to let this boy off—perhaps we need to make an example out of him. It's what your father would have done."

Her teeth itched at the mention of her father, but she wasn't about to air family laundry in the mayor's office.

"He's the wrong kid for that," she said. "The last two kids we sent over to DOC came back worse."

"You know, I hired you because I knew you would change the department. And you have—in the six months you've been here, you've done great work, Chief."

Juliette blinked, the compliment sideswiping her. "Thank you, Mayor," she said, feeling a hot blush inch its way up her neck.

"But there's only so much leeway I can give you before people start to notice," he said. "People are used to the way your father did things. And you're coming real close to blurring the lines of your job."

"Like you said, it's a small town, Mayor. People already notice, they just don't care." She glanced pointedly at his empty glass of Alka-Seltzer and lifted one eyebrow.

A poker game, in a church of all places, and the whole town knew and let it slide.

They stared at each other for a long moment and Juliette wondered if maybe she'd overstepped—he was the mayor, for crying out loud.

But then he laughed and Juliette nearly sagged with relief. "You're right. But this kid gets brought in one more time—even if it's for milk and cookies—and I'm going to start to care. And that ain't good for either of you." He didn't bother veiling the threat. "You ready to risk your job over this kid?"

"It won't come to that, sir," she said.

"I certainly hope not." He looked back down at his desk. "Thank you, Chief."

"Thank you," she said before turning to leave.

"How did it go with Tyler, when he found out the boy tried to steal his car?" he asked before she got to the door.

"He's not pressing charges." She shrugged. "So, pretty well."

"I have to say, I'm surprised. The boy named the damn car."

The boy, she thought bitterly, *probably named his damn penis.*

"Well," she said with a tight smile. "Tyler has always been one for surprises."

"SOMEBODY'S POUNDING ON the door, son," Richard said, from the other couch in the library. They'd passed out here after searching the room for gems. Well, after Dad had searched for gems.

Tyler had dedicated himself to the systematic emptying of a whiskey bottle.

"I hear them," Tyler said, pushing a pillow over his eyes to block out the morning sun.

"You need to answer that."

"You answer it."

"What if it's that cop?" Richard said. "You want to explain me?"

No. No, he did not.

Tyler stood, got his bearings, and stumbled to the front door.

"Someone better be dead," he muttered, opening the door only to find the kid—what's his name, with the beat-up face?—staring up at him.

"Miguel?" Tyler asked, the name erupting from the fog in his brain. He carefully kept the door closed around him so Miguel couldn't see inside. No need for the kid to see Richard. "What are you doing here?" Tyler asked. "You... okay?"

Miguel nodded, pushing back the gray hood of his sweatshirt, revealing bruises and the burn that looked no better for having been twenty-four hours older.

Tyler stepped out onto the porch and shut the door firmly behind him. "What can I do for you, Miguel?"

"I wanted to say I'm sorry," Miguel said. "About your car."

Tyler was a little stunned. The hoodlum apologizes? He hadn't seen that coming. "Bad idea stealing cars," he said, because he figured some kind of anti-grand theft auto PSA was called for.

"I guess so," Miguel said, glancing over at the road, the big tree in front.

Tyler waited, but the kid didn't seem to be in any kind of hurry to elaborate.

"Well," Tyler said, clapping his hands together, hoping Miguel might startle like a bird, "glad we got that sorted out—"

"I wouldn't need to steal any cars if I had money," Miguel said.

Tyler's jaw dropped. "Excuse me?"

"I saw you on TV last year winning all that money," Miguel said. Tyler's head cleared real fast. Extortion. He hadn't seen that coming, either. This kid was full of surprises.

"I don't want your money," Miguel said, correctly reading the fury Tyler was projecting. "I'm not here for that."

"Then why are you here?"

"I want to learn how to do what you do," Miguel said.

"Play cards?" Tyler laughed.

Miguel nodded, not laughing at all. Tyler laughed harder. The kid was *serious?* He wondered if Dad had heard that, because he would have gotten a real kick out of it.

"That's a good one, Miguel. Seriously. But—"

"I already know how to play. I play online over at my friend George's house and I win. A lot."

"That's great, but I'm not teaching you how to play poker. Juliette would have a fit."

"She doesn't have to know."

Tyler reassessed the kid in front of him. His dark eyes, past the scabby blood and bruises, were focused, smart and…very, very old.

A kid who'd never been a kid.

The sound of a car pulling around the corner, spitting gravel, ripped Tyler's eyes from Miguel's.

The car was too far away to tell who it was, but suddenly the cherry top blazed once from just inside the windshield.

Juliette. Holy hell.

"Listen," Miguel said. "Just let me come here after school, a few hours for a few weeks. That's it."

"That's *it?*" Tyler asked, laughing.

Juliette's car stopped in front of the house and she was out the door in a split second, marching toward them.

"Morning, Juliette," Tyler said, waving as though it was all no big deal, when under his shirt he had a good cold sweat going.

"We got a call saying some kid was snooping around here," Juliette snapped.

His father! He must have been peeking through the window, but what was he thinking, calling the cops? Juliette would be furious if she found out Richard had been the one sneaking around the place when no one was around.

"Sorry to call," Tyler said, falling in step with the lie because he had no choice. "I saw someone snooping around, I got a little nervous and—"

"You!" she said, sticking her finger in Miguel's face, not even listening to Tyler's crappy cover-up. "You should be at school."

"I show up like this and Ms. Jenkins has to call the social workers," he said, and she rocked back for a second. She took a deep breath, as if reassessing, and Tyler got the sense that Juliette was flying blind.

"George is bringing me my homework," Miguel said in the vacuum. "He told Ms. Jenkins I was sick. Don't worry, Chief, I've got it covered."

"Then what are you doing here?"

"He came to apologize," Tyler said. "About the car. Very adult of him, if you ask me."

Juliette watched Tyler for a long time, her eyes unreadable. And he had the worst, the *worst* urge to reach over, touch her shoulder and tell her everything would be fine.

But he had the old man to hide, some stolen gems to find, a delinquent to get rid of and a whole lot of past experience that told him reaching out for Juliette only hurt in the end.

"Fine," she finally said, holding out her arm as if to steer

Miguel out toward her car. "You apologized. If you're not going to be at school, you can come down to the station. Get to work cleaning cars."

Miguel stepped away but glanced back at Tyler, who did nothing but squirm under the kid's intense gaze.

He tried hard not to see the desperation in Miguel's old-man eyes, but then remembered that Miguel had a little sister.

A little sister he was trying to protect.

All too clearly, Tyler recalled being sixteen and feeling sixty, trying to keep a little sister safe, keep her a child, when his entire world was conspiring to rip her innocence away from her.

And then there was Juliette, working so hard against a system set up to ruin kids like Miguel. And while he wasn't about to teach Miguel how to play poker, he could find something to keep the kid busy a few hours a day.

Before he could put the brakes on this ludicrous idea, he jumped right off the cliff.

"I think I figured out what you could do to punish Miguel here."

"Oh, you did, did you?" Juliette asked.

"I did." He nodded, not a single idea coming to him. "I had an idea." Tyler kept nodding.

"Okay, so let's hear it." Juliette shifted her weight and the porch groaned. The sagging, beat-up porch.

"He's going to fix up the house," Tyler said.

"Not buying it, Tyler," she said, shaking her head. "Let's go, Miguel."

"What do you mean, not buying it?" he asked, his temper flaring. "I'm trying to help you out!"

"Well, I don't need your help." She practically sneered, and Tyler threw his hands up.

"This is what I get for trying to be a good guy."

"Oh, please, Tyler. Like you would know?"

"But, I want to do this," Miguel said, before Tyler could say anything. "He said he would supervise, he'd even write up reports and stuff."

Tyler blinked down at the kid. The word *supervise* had never even crossed his brain. Miguel shrugged and smiled, and damn if Tyler didn't start liking the kid.

"Right." Juliette's sarcasm was not missed by Tyler. "Tyler O'Neill supervising is a disaster waiting to happen."

"Hey," Tyler said, "you don't know that."

"I know you, Tyler, and that's enough. This isn't going to happen. Now, come on, Miguel. You can come willingly to the station, or I'll drag your ass to school. Come what may."

Miguel followed Juliette back across the yard and Tyler watched them from his rotting porch.

You dodged a bullet there, man, he told himself.

But oddly, the sting in his chest felt like disappointment.

IMAGINING THE STEERING WHEEL was Tyler's neck didn't give Juliette much satisfaction, but she couldn't quite stop squeezing the plastic. Not two days in this town and Tyler was tearing apart the little seams that kept her life together. All she needed was Tyler knocking on her father's door to make the chaos complete.

Why in the world were the men in her life always like land mines?

"What are you going to do?" Miguel asked, petulant in the backseat, a little dog thwarted. She had no idea what had brought Miguel and Tyler together, but it didn't take a psychic to see where it would lead.

"Did you go to his house?" she asked, watching him in the rearview mirror.

"Yes," Miguel said.

"This was all your idea?"

"Better than cleaning cop cars at the station."

The kid was creative, she'd give him that.

She pulled up in front of the station just in time to see Mayor Bourdage climb out of his pickup, a stack of files under his arm.

Her stomach fell and twisted into her shoes.

"Duck," she said.

"What?"

"Get down!"

Miguel slouched in the backseat and Juliette watched the mayor climb the steps and go in the glass doors. She waited a few seconds and then called Lisa.

"Bonne Terre Police," Lisa said. "How can—"

"Lisa—"

"Jul—"

"Shh," Juliette hissed. "Is the mayor standing there?"

"No, I sent him into your office."

"Why is he here?"

"Squad cars or something."

Juliette rested her head against the steering wheel. Tyler O'Neill, she thought. If given half a chance, she was going to kill the man.

"Tell him I'm running late, I'll be right back." Juliette ended the call and threw her phone into the passenger seat. Then, despite being police chief and having an impressionable minor in the car, Juliette swore as hard and as long and as creatively as she could.

When she finished, she turned the car around and headed back to The Manor and Tyler O'Neill and what was surely going to be the biggest mistake of her life.

"WHAT ARE YOU DOING, BOY?" Richard asked, stomping through the library and into the kitchen. "Telling the police you want the kid here?"

"Dad." Tyler sighed, rubbing his forehead. He had a headache pounding right behind his eyes, induced partly from yesterday's whiskey and partly from the delightful wake-up call. "Why did you call the cops? I had it handled."

"Right, handled. Like you handle everything—"

Tyler stood, sick to death of the criticism coming from every corner. "Don't start with me, Dad. Don't you dare."

"We've got a fortune in gems around here, Tyler, and you're—"

"Handling it!" he yelled.

A furious pounding at the front door ended the fight before it began.

"What now?" Dad asked.

"Tyler!" Juliette's voice, muffled by wood and glass, still managed to stop his heart. "Open the door!"

CHAPTER SIX

IT WAS LIKE *THE TWILIGHT ZONE* or something. A man comes back to his hometown with the intention of staying at an empty house and before he knows it he's saddled with his father, a juvenile would-be car thief and his…whatever the hell Juliette was to him—old girlfriend, first love, giant pain in various body parts.

"I will be checking up on him," Juliette said, looking stony-eyed and serious. She sized Tyler up and he felt as though he'd just been measured for his coffin. "Every day."

"I don't think that's nece—"

"And you," Juliette talked over him like he wasn't there, turning all her attention to Miguel. "You will go to school tomorrow. Tell Ms. Jenkins you were in a fight with the football team or something, I don't care. But you're at school and then you're here and I'll make sure," she said. "And if you're so much as ten minutes—"

"I won't be," Miguel said, quick and eager, looking nothing like the ballsy kid who'd been on his stoop this morning. Now he was all exuberant puppy, bright-eyed and wagging tail.

Seriously, Tyler thought, what the hell is going on here?

"No funny stuff," Juliette said to Tyler and some kind of wiseass comment was right on the tip of his tongue, some kind of "screw you" because she was authority after all, despite being Juliette. He really did have this thing with people telling him what to do, but then she went and blinked and those wide hazel eyes weren't so steely, weren't so tough. "I'm counting on you, Tyler. And you've got to know how hard that is for me."

I know, he thought. *I broke your heart. I hurt you and hurt you again.*

Maybe it was shame, maybe it was her eyes, or maybe it was the overly optimistic vibe coming off the kid, but whatever it was his smart-ass joke died on his lips and he nodded.

"I promise, Juliette. I really do."

She snorted, her doubt like a whole other person standing on the porch, shaking its head at him.

"I'll come here right after school tomorrow," Miguel said. The kid was actually smiling—well, as much as he could without popping stitches.

He thinks he's won, Tyler thought. But that old saying about conning a con was poignantly true in this situation, particularly when the con happened to involve a house in terrible need of fixing up.

There would be no card playing, not even Go Fish. But the boy would work.

"This is totally nuts," Juliette muttered. "I'm gonna lose my job over this garbage."

"Everything will be cool," Miguel said. The earnestness in the kid's voice watered Tyler's shame, made it grow a little more.

"It will be," he added his own weak assurances.

Her eyes bounced between them and she shook her head. "I'm crazy. I'm absolutely out of my mind," she said, and turned, walking across the lawn to her car.

Tyler stood next to the kid, watching her go, marveling

at the way the world worked, how in Bonne Terre, the joke was always on him.

This was his own fault, he'd actually suggested the idea. Was he insane? A no-account gambler in charge of a juvenile delinquent?

I'd kill a cactus, he thought, flabbergasted. Four years ago, he had to give away a dog because the basic care and maintenance of another living thing was just too much for him. He lived in a hotel for crying out loud.

He looked at the kid.

What am I going to do with you?

"So?" Miguel said once Juliette's taillights vanished down the road. The boy rubbed his hands together as if he was about to sit down to a feast of gambling delights. "Where do we start? Five card? Texas hold 'em?"

Tyler made a big point of looking at the front of the house. He flicked off some of the peeling white paint, examined the sad and neglected windowsills and bounced on a few of the sagging floorboards on the porch.

Dad was going to blow a gasket, no doubt about it, but Tyler didn't see a way around this.

"The porch," he said, grinning at the kid's crestfallen expression. "I do believe we'll start with the porch."

"What are you talking about?" the kid asked, following him through the red door into the shadowed foyer. "I'm here to learn how to play cards."

"Yeah, but I liked my idea better."

"I'm not going to fix up your house," Miguel said, stopping and crossing his arms in the hallway. Tyler turned.

"Then maybe I should call Juliette and tell her it's off? You can wash cars at the station."

"No way, man, a deal is a deal."

"What the hell is going on here?" Richard demanded, stepping into the hallway from the dark library.

"Dad, don't freak out—"

"Don't freak out? There's a kid in this house, and from what it sounds like, he's going to be here a while."

"Who the hell is this guy?" Miguel asked, suddenly a little gangster.

"No one," Tyler said, "ignore him."

"He's not staying," Richard insisted.

Tyler looked steadily at his father, balancing all his impulses to strangle him. "I don't have a choice," he bit out, "You called the cops."

"Maybe I should just tell the chief that your dad don't want me here," Miguel said.

Tyler rubbed his eyes, his face, ran his fingers through his hair, wishing he were back at the Bellagio with nothing more stressful than a massage to schedule.

"Miguel," he sighed, putting his cards on the table, "you can't tell Juliette about my dad. This whole thing will blow up if you do."

"Then maybe you should teach me some cards—"

"Oh," Richard said, brightening at the idea of an enthusiastic young pupil. "If this is about poker—"

"It's not," Tyler said to his father. "We're not teaching him the game. Ever."

"Fine," Richard said, heading into the kitchen, "but you better keep him out of the house and out of our way."

Miguel's face was all but glowing, the prospect of blackmail no doubt warming the little cockles of his devious heart.

"Let me stop you before you even get started." Tyler chuckled and put his hand on Miguel's stiff shoulder. "You don't want to be at that station. Even if I'm not teaching you cards, you'd rather be here. You tipped your hand, kid. I've seen every card you've got."

He watched the kid digest it, the wheels turning behind those bright eyes.

"Now," Tyler said, his throat suddenly dry, his hands wet. Bluffing was nothing—he did it in his sleep, ordering breakfast, every single conversation with every other person in his life was mostly a bluff—but with Juliette in the mix, he wasn't on his game. He couldn't keep a clear head.

But Juliette could not know about his father.

"We can call Juliette and we can both of us tell her what's happening. I'll tell her you just want to learn to gamble and you can tell her about my dad. But she already expects the worst of me. She's driving away right now pretty sure I'm lying to her. But if I'm forced to tell her that you're making all this up—it'll hurt her."

The boy swallowed, swore under his breath and Tyler could see that the idea of hurting Juliette bothered him.

So young, that kid, still so many people to disappoint and hurt. Years of doling out pain to people who might trust him, or God forbid love him, stretched out ahead of Miguel.

But it was obvious Miguel wasn't going to start today, and he wasn't going to start with Juliette.

Points to Miguel. He was way up on Tyler.

There was a stab of pain in his chest, a wish that he could go back and feel that way again. Clean. Redeemable. Tyler could barely remember what doing the right thing felt like.

"So, what?" Miguel asked. "I'm just gonna clean up your porch?"

"Yeah." Tyler grinned. "And maybe my windowsills."

Tyler led the boy through the old house, listening to him whistle under his breath as they stepped under the giant chandelier.

"What is this place?" Miguel asked.

"A relic," Tyler answered. He led the boy through the inner courtyard, manicured and pristine as a golf course.

"Whoa," the kid breathed and Tyler smiled. Shabby on the outside, but the old girl still had it where it counted. "This is like a mansion or something?"

"It was," Tyler answered. They stepped through the second set of doors, into the back part of the house, and he rested his hand on the brass doorknob leading to the back courtyard. "This place used to be a brothel," he said and the kid snorted. "I'm not kidding. My great-great-great-grandfather built it. It's been in my family for hundreds of years."

Miguel nodded. "That's cool."

"It is. It is very cool, so you can imagine how I'd feel if anything happened to this place—"

"What are you saying?" Miguel asked, hot and bothered.

"I'm saying—to the kid who tried to steal my car—" Tyler arched his eyebrow and let that sink in "—don't get any ideas."

"My idea was learning how to play cards so I could make some money, now I'm slave labor—"

"I'll pay you," Tyler said, because that thing about the money bothered Tyler. He knew the kid needed out, needed a way to take care of his sister, and Tyler remembered feeling that way all too well. "But that's between you and me. Juliette doesn't need to know."

Miguel nodded in agreement and Tyler felt a shimmery satisfaction at doing the right thing.

"Now," Tyler said, opening the door to the rear courtyard—the one that was truly magical, even to a jade like him. "Let's get some tools and go to work."

But the kid barely heard him. He stared wide-eyed and

slack jawed at the maze and the whirling fountain, the glittering glass roof of the greenhouse.

Tyler walked past him, smiling, to the toolshed in the back corner. Tyler swung open the wooden door to the dusty interior of the shed and the smell of grass and dirt flooded out, giving him the weird desire to actually get his hands dirty.

Miguel caught up and took the tools Tyler started to hand him. A couple of scrappers, a crowbar, a sledgehammer. Tyler tucked a few pairs of dirty canvas gloves into his back pocket.

"Hey, how come you've got such a nice yard and your house looks like crap?"

"An excellent question," Tyler said. "I think we were just waiting for the right extortionist to come along."

"You think you're funny, don't you?"

"Sometimes," Tyler said.

"What's the story with you and the chief?" Miguel asked.

"What do you mean?" Tyler asked, playing dumb as he stepped back out into the sunshine.

"Why does she expect the worst from you?"

Tyler kicked the door shut behind him.

"Because that's all I've ever given her."

JULIETTE HELD OPEN HER office door, a slice of sunshine leading the mayor into the squad room like an illuminated arrow.

"Thanks again, Mayor, for coming in this morning," she said, feeling that their little meeting had gone well, that perhaps things might start to go her way. Maybe her whole career, a big chunk of her life, wasn't circling the drain.

"My pleasure," Mayor Bourdage said. "Now I'm going

to go get the paperwork underway for that new squad car so you can finally stop badgering me."

"Well, if this is how you reward bad behavior I'm going to get the wrong idea."

They both laughed, the good will between them something she could practically taste. A sweetness that barely covered the bitter taste of his distrust over Miguel. Mayor Bourdage had brought it up again at the beginning of the meeting.

Hard to believe, but taking Miguel back to Tyler had been the right thing to do.

She turned toward the door and stopped at the sight of her father, Jasper Tremblant, standing at the night shift desk, talking to Owens.

"Dad!"

"Juliette," her dad cried. His smile was wide, but his dark eyes gave him away. They bounced between her and the mayor, sizing things up, always watching. Measuring every relationship, every moment, convinced all the time that there was something else going on under the surface, something deceitful. Something rotten.

Thirty years as a cop does that to a man, I suppose, Juliette thought.

The mayor made his departure, leaving her mostly alone with her father.

"What are you doing here?" she asked, leaning in and kissing his smooth dark cheek.

"A father can't take his daughter to lunch?" he asked and Juliette glanced down at her watch—a bit early for lunch. Now she was the one wondering what was going on under the surface.

"Are you checking up on me?" she asked, trying to make it a joke, when it was anything but. Especially with Owens looking on.

"Always, my dear, always." He, too, tried to make it a joke, but she wasn't laughing. "Now, how about a tuna melt from Carver's?"

"Sounds great," she said, through her teeth. "Just give me a second." She pointed to Owens, whose smile faded. "In my office. Now."

"I SWEAR," OWENS SAID, after she'd accused him of breaking the chain of command and giving the mayor Miguel's file. "I didn't do it."

"I don't believe you, Owens," she said. "And that's actually worse than if you did do it, do you understand that?" She looked hard at him, willing to get it through his big thick head that he was jeopardizing his career. "I don't trust you. I'm your boss and I don't trust you."

"I haven't done anything—"

She slammed her desk drawer shut, the rattle and bang silencing him. "You've been skirting insubordination since I was hired and you think your years on the force are going to keep you safe." she shook her head and stood up, leaning over the desk. "But they won't."

"You can't fire—"

"Out of respect for your wife who deserves better than you, no, I won't fire you." Her father would be screaming his head off right now, but Nell Owens was on dialysis and they counted on the force's insurance. "But this is going to be the second letter of discipline in your file and you're out of rotation for three weeks."

"What?"

"You'll be on dispatch."

Owens bit down hard on his lip, his cheeks red, nearly purple.

"Something else you wanted to say?" she asked, blinking at him.

He shook his head and left, and when the door slammed shut behind him she sank down in her chair. Benching Owens was the right thing to do, and she felt pretty good doing it. Damn good, if she was honest. But Owens was walking out of here with a grudge, and stupid men with grudges did stupid things.

How, she wondered, *is this going to bite me in the ass?*

There was a knock on her door and her dad poked his head in. His tight salt-and-pepper curls were the only real indication of his age, but under that perfect mocha skin she'd inherited and that thin, athletic body was a weak heart. A heart that doctors had warned him couldn't hold up to the stress of police work.

Doctors told Dad to quit. To take up golf. Yoga.

"Everything okay?" he asked, his eyes sincere for the moment.

"Owens is forgetting the basic rules regarding chain of command," she said.

"Can't have that."

"No," she said. "I can't." She waited with a half a breath for him to tell her how to do her job. How she should have put him out on the street.

"You know, honey, we do things differently, but you run a tight ship here. I'd hate to see that jeopardized."

The compliment sent all of her warning flags waving.

Dad was not one for compliments.

And then, like a lightning bolt, she realized why Dad was really here—he must have heard Tyler was in town. He was checking up on her, making sure the past didn't go repeating itself.

"Why are you here, Dad?" she asked. "Really?"

"Lunch with my baby isn't enough?"

"Sure," she said, and crossed her arms over her chest. "If

I believed that was the only thing that brought you down here today."

Jasper turned and shut the door. "I heard Tyler O'Neill was back in town."

"Is that so?" She wasn't exactly sure where this anger came from, but it was here and it was growing.

"I know you know," he said. "And I just wanted—" Dad shrugged gracefully "—to make sure everything was as it should be."

"Meaning?"

"You're a good chief. But that boy is bad news. I don't trust you when he's around."

She chewed on her lips, wishing she could argue, but frankly it was the truth. Her truth. Her secret shameful reality. Tyler O'Neill had her number.

"What are you suggesting I do?" she asked.

"Make sure he doesn't plan on staying too long."

"You want me to run him out? Gather a posse and drive him out of town?"

Jasper stared at his daughter, the weight of his gaze and his expectations and love nearly crushing her. "You never did see clearly when it came to that boy."

"I see just fine, Dad," she said. "He's in town checking on The Manor and will probably be gone by the end of next week."

Again, that casual shrug that managed to say so much and so little at the same time. That shrug had thrown her off balance her entire life, had made her feel unsteady even as a kid. "Then everything is fine."

"Just fine," she agreed, still angry.

"Then let's go get that tuna melt," Jasper said, his smile wide, his eyes warm. But it was too late. The chill of her father's love had seeped into her bones.

CHAPTER SEVEN

"THIS IS POINTLESS," Tyler sighed, squirting a mountain of soap into his hands at the kitchen sink. There was a reason why there were so few basements in Louisiana—everything got wet and never ever dried out. Half the boxes down there were black with mold, the other half were practically disintegrating. Truth was, he spent most of the time he was supposed to be searching for gems just cleaning the place out.

But it was Thursday night, and after three days of searching for the gems, he was getting tired of pretending to care.

He heard his dad clomping up the stairs.

"The gems aren't down there, Dad," Tyler said before he could start complaining that Tyler was giving up.

"I think you're right," Richard said as he stepped up from the basement stairs into the hallway outside the kitchen. Spiderwebs dusted his hair. "But we haven't checked the attic. Or Margot's room—"

"You're not going in Margot's room," Tyler insisted, the very idea giving him the creeps. He could only humor his father so far.

Richard rolled his eyes and pulled open the fridge. "What we need is to recruit that Miguel kid—"

"Not an option."

"Come on, it's been three days and he's barely managed

to tear down half the porch. He'd be better put to use inside the house."

Tyler leaned over the door of the fridge, making eye contact with his dad. "Stay away from him, Dad."

"Oh, I'm a bad influence? And you're what…Mother Teresa? What would be worse, teaching the kid poker or having him look for the gems?"

Tyler laughed. "They're about equal," he said. "Juliette would kill me either way."

Richard stood up in the open V of the fridge door. "This Juliette…who the hell is she?"

Right. Like he was going to tell Dad.

He reached around the old man and grabbed a beer. "She's the police chief—I think that's enough reason not to get her angry."

"Cut the bullshit," Richard said, shutting the door and leaning up against the far counter with a beer of his own. A sly grin crawled across his face. "Who is she to you? I watch every day when she comes and picks up that kid, and you don't act like she's no one. She gets out of that car and you look like the only woman left in the world just stepped onto the grass. So, son, who is she to you?"

Tyler twisted the cap off the beer before taking a long slug of it, trying to swallow down the strange urge to tell Richard. To confide in someone, anyone, his father, for crying out loud—the pain he felt every damn day when Juliette showed up to pick up Miguel.

How when Tyler looked at her, the weight of the mistakes he'd made nearly crushed him. And worse, infinitely painfully worse, was the way possibilities hung in the air around her like fireflies in tall grass.

"We…ah…we had a thing. A long time ago."

"Ah," Dad said, as if he was a daytime talk show host. "A thing?"

Tyler pursed his lips. "It was nothing."

"She what sent you to Las Vegas?"

He felt that stab of memory, the pain no less intense ten years down the road. He'd loved her and he'd left her and it had been like tearing apart his body.

"In a way," he said. "But nothing's there anymore."

"Oh!" Richard said, laughing long and hard. "Oh, son, that's a good one. Try selling it to some other sucker."

"Didn't you ever want something normal, Dad?" Tyler asked, knowing it would get him nowhere. "A home?"

"Home?" Richard said. "I tried that," he said, and shuddered dramatically.

"Aren't you ever tired of being alone?"

"I'm not alone," Richard said, his grin wide and white and perfect, a man with no cares in the world. "I am never, ever alone, I've got friends—"

"Friends who implicate you in credit-card fraud," he said. "Are they really your friends? Can you count on them? Do they know you?"

"No," Richard said, the answer apparently needed no thought, no contemplation. "I have you for that. Just like you have me. We know each other because we're the same. You know, maybe we *should* go back to Vegas. I knew having that boy around was going to cause trouble."

Tyler shook his head. "This has nothing to do with Miguel. Trust me."

Richard narrowed his eyes as if staring at Tyler from a long ways away. "This about that cop? The woman?"

"Maybe," he answered. Maybe definitely.

"Women are trouble, Tyler," Richard said, his voice ominous.

"Not all of them," he said. He thought of Margot and

Savannah. Of Juliette. Some women were gifts. Gifts that you didn't recognize until it was too late.

"If we're not going to search for gems, I'm going to take a shower."

Tyler heard it all from a hundred miles away, lost in some dark and desolate place. Alone. Always alone. Thoughts of Juliette stirred the ghosts in his head.

And he knew, without a doubt, he didn't want to become his father, casual and hurtful, without a place to call home.

Without someone to love him back.

FRIDAY AFTERNOON, TYLER was done babysitting his father and had moved on to babysitting his juvenile delinquent, which was by far the more preferred gig.

Despite the kid's attitude.

Or maybe because of it.

It was hard to say.

"You want to get off your butt and help me, Tyler?"

Tyler leisurely turned the page of the newspaper, stretched out his legs then settled a little deeper into his lawn chair. "Not particularly. You tried to steal my car. I'm holding a grudge."

Miguel pushed the skinny edge of the crowbar under the last of the rotten floorboards and leaned into it, pushing as hard as he could until finally the wood splintered, cracked and flew off into the lawn.

Barely missing Tyler's head.

"Hey!" Tyler yelled, wiping the sun tea he'd spilled down his shirt. "Watch it. I told you, Miguel, you've got to be more careful."

"And I told you I don't know how to do this crap!" Miguel yelled back. "Show me what to do!"

Tyler laughed, rubbing salt in poor Miguel's wounds.

Honestly, the kid was so much fun to get a rise out of. "What makes you think I know how to do this shit?"

Miguel swore at him in Spanish but Tyler only swore back.

The boy couldn't hold a silent grudge, and within minutes he was yammering on again.

"So," Miguel said, kicking aside some pieces of porch. "When you had those two aces you had no idea that the Japanese dude had a straight."

Tyler turned the page, hiding his grin behind the sports section. Every day Miguel had some kind of question for him about that World Series of Poker game. The kid must go home and study the clip on YouTube.

"You ask your teachers as many questions as you do me?"

Miguel shot him a give-me-a-break look while wedging the crowbar under another board.

"I'm just saying, if you cared about your books as much as you care about gambling, you could go to college, stop busting up porches for a living."

"This is hardly a living," Miguel said. "You're barely paying me minimum wage."

Tyler swatted at a small yellow butterfly that hovered around him. Nature, so…annoying.

"Did you go to college?" Miguel asked.

"No," Tyler lied—well, partly lied. He didn't graduate college.

"So, you're doing all right?"

"There's more to life than money, Miguel," Tyler said quietly, folding the paper carefully along its crease. Not that he expected Miguel to believe that; Tyler certainly hadn't believed it when he was Miguel's age. It takes a whole lot of money to make you realize what you can and can't buy with it.

"Says the guy driving a Porsche," Miguel scoffed.

Tyler turned his head to look at Sweet Suzy sitting under the late-afternoon sun. She was a pretty wicked car. But this car, his whole damn lifestyle, came at a price. And these days he felt that price keenly, a bitter knife in his gut.

"I bought that car with my first big win," he said.

"Yeah?" Miguel ran his eyes across Suzy's curves like a sixteen-year-old should, like the Porsche was a woman full grown.

"I've had to sell her twice," he said. "When I lost it all. I sold her so I could have food to eat. A roof over my head."

"But you've got her now," Miguel said.

"Yep, each time I bought her back for about double what I sold her for. Suzy's cost me a fortune."

"Why didn't you just buy a new car?" Miguel asked.

"She's a reminder."

"Of what?" Miguel said.

"That being a gambler is no way to live."

"I don't get it," Miguel said. "You're rich as hell."

"Right now," Tyler said. "I could go back to Vegas and lose it all tomorrow. And probably will."

"But you're good."

"That's not a guarantee of anything," he said, the truth undeniable. "I've beaten the best players in the world and I've been beaten by grandmas playing with their pensions. Being good doesn't mean anything against luck."

"I still don't understand what's wrong with teaching me a few tricks. It's not like I'm asking you to teach me how to cheat."

"That's good, because I don't cheat."

Miguel kept working the porch, hopefully thinking about his career options and not how he could steal Suzy again, and Tyler went back to his paper.

The sun had dipped down below the chimney and that's when Juliette usually came around to pick up Miguel.

He braced himself for the other part of his day.

The Juliette part.

Equal measures torture and bliss.

Her voice, both soft and rough, like rubbing up against velvet the wrong way, had the ability to make Miguel jerk upright, all but saluting.

Made parts of Tyler want to salute, too.

And yesterday she'd worn a green jacket with khaki pants that made her legs look a mile long. The color of the jacket made her eyes more green than brown and they practically glowed against the gorgeous mocha of her skin.

Today he was hoping for a skirt. A short one.

No matter what, she was beautiful and real and so full of hate toward him it made his skin hurt just being close to her.

"Excuse me," a woman's sharp voice said from behind him and Tyler turned in his chair, shielding his eyes from the remaining daylight.

A woman stood there, a black shadow against the low blaze of the setting sun, but he could tell already that she was the kind of woman that made his balls curl up into his belly for warmth.

"Can I help you?" he asked, standing up to face the older woman, hoping, truly hoping, this had nothing to do with his father.

"My name is Nora Sullivan. I'm from the Beauregard Parish Office of Community Services." She pulled a card from the front pocket of a charcoal pantsuit that made her look like a big gray box and handed it to Tyler. "I'm looking for Miguel Pastor."

Tyler took the card, his neck tingling, a terrible foreboding that what was happening here was bad. Very bad.

All he could do was stall, so he took his time reading the card and then shoved it in his back pocket.

"I'm Tyler O'Neill," he said, getting his hand crushed in the woman's vice grip. "And Miguel is—" Tyler turned back around but the porch was empty, the crowbar lying in the grass.

Miguel was gone.

"Not here at the moment," he said quickly, panic beating its wings against his chest.

"Our office got a call that he is usually here after school in some kind of community service capacity. And that there was some concern about the boy's recent experience with local police."

There were a few times in Tyler's life when he was literally struck dumb. This was one of those times.

"You really need to talk to Police Chief Tremblant about that," he said lamely.

"So I'm gathering," she said. She checked her watch and pulled out another card. "I've left her a message at the station, but I'm on my way over to Calcasieu DOC. If you see her, can you have her call me?"

"You bet," he said, perhaps a bit too eagerly. Nora Sullivan watched him with cagey dark eyes. Eyes that had seen every trick in the book.

Tyler felt about thirteen again.

Nora nodded and left, crossing the wide front lawn to her sedan parked at the curb. He waited until she was gone before running through the house, yelling Miguel's name.

No sign of the kid. Not even Richard had seen him.

He grabbed his phone and dialed Juliette's number with fingers that shook.

DRIVING FROM THE STATION to The Manor on Friday afternoon, Juliette actually felt the steel girders holding her spine in place relax. The metal bands squeezing her forehead had loosened and the headache blazing behind her eyes had faded to a small flame. A small manageable flame.

It was working. This ludicrous plan was actually working.

It had been four days, and so far Tyler and Miguel had torn down most of a porch and that was it. Tyler hadn't taken Miguel to a strip club, or taught him how to gamble. Miguel went to school every day and then showed up at The Manor and did the work he was supposed to and Louisa was staying at a friend's house after school until Juliette and Miguel picked her up.

Dr. Roberts hadn't had a change of heart and called in the social workers and neither had Mayor Bourdage. The guys in the station were going about their business.

Even Tyler had kept his mouth shut.

Everything was working, except for the fact that she didn't know what to do next. Father Michaels ran a drug program from the church on Thursday nights, but Miguel didn't do drugs.

She'd called the Calcasieu Parish juvenile parole officer, who hadn't been much help. Not a huge surprise, considering Miguel wasn't in the system.

Preventing kids from getting into the system was what she was trying to do.

It was times like these when she could use her father's advice, and she wished there wasn't a mile deep chasm between their philosophies.

Her phone rang beside her and Tyler's name popped up on her screen. The same rush of hot and cold that she'd been living with for the past week rolled over her. It was so strange to simultaneously hate someone and remember every single filthy thing he'd ever done to her.

She felt torn in two by Tyler. She'd gone into this whole arrangement waiting for him to disappoint her. Knowing it was only a matter of time before he jerked some rug out from under her.

And every day that he didn't was both a blessing and a curse.

"Chief Tremblant," she said, answering her phone and keeping things official.

"Juliette," Tyler said, his voice scraping across her nerve endings, lighting up dark parts of her body. "We have a problem."

"He's gone?" she asked ten minutes later on Tyler's front lawn.

"I turned around for a second, I swear." To his credit, Tyler looked a bit freaked out. Wild-eyed and worried, which wasn't helping the state of her nerves. If Tyler O'Neill was worried, the world was about to end. "He must have run when he saw the social worker coming."

Social worker. Juliette glanced down at the card in her hand. Nora Sullivan. Child Welfare Investigator/Counselor.

Miguel, I'm so sorry.

So much for this ludicrous plan working. She felt the consequences of her decisions like a two-ton rock rolling downhill right at her. Her career, her life—everything was about to go splat.

The girders were back, her brain being squeezed to mush by the metal bands.

"My car is here, so he's on foot," Tyler said. "We should leave now—"

"I think I know where he is. Give me a second," she said, and pulled out her cell phone. Her first call was to the friend with whom Louisa was staying. Miguel wasn't going anywhere without Louisa.

"Patricia," she said, and switched to Spanish when the older woman answered. "Has Miguel picked up Louisa?"

"No, Chief Tremblant. Louisa is here alone."

"When Miguel comes, please keep him there until I come get him," she said. "It's very important that you don't let him leave."

"Sí, señorita."

Juliette hung up and contemplated the card in her hand. Nora Sullivan. Juliette took a deep breath. She didn't need to be forced to be accountable. She'd gone into this situation with her eyes wide-open. The mistakes were hers—so, then, would be the punishment.

She dialed the number and—thank God—got an answering machine.

"Hi, Ms. Sullivan," she said, keeping her voice tight, "this is Police Chief Juliette Tremblant over in Bonne Terre. I'd like to make an appointment with you to discuss Miguel Pastor at your earliest convenience. Please give me a call Monday morning at this number. Thank you."

She hung up and rubbed at her forehead. The pain was killing her. She wished she could just go home, pull down the shades and find a dark corner to lick her wounds.

But that wasn't her style. Not anymore. Not since Tyler had left.

Tyler.

She turned, all her frustration and anger searching for a vent and a worthy victim.

And there was none so worthy as Tyler O'Neill.

CHAPTER EIGHT

TYLER COULD TELL JULIETTE'S fuse was lit and she was a live bomb looking for a place to explode.

And it's gonna be all over me, he thought, resigned to it. Thinking, actually, that he deserved it. He'd lost the kid, after all.

This whole thing had been a bad idea. He had no business getting involved with Miguel and Juliette. It had only been a matter of time before he screwed this up, too.

"Miguel's going to be fine," she told him and he was dumbfounded for the moment. Thank God.

"Is there anything else you haven't told me?" she asked in full-on cop mode, putting his teeth on edge. "Something you might have forgotten?"

"Miguel and I were talking," he said. "And the social worker just showed up—"

"What were you talking about?"

Tyler blinked, knowing what this was going to do to her temper. "What in the world does that have to do with anything?"

"She probably overheard you—"

"She didn't," he insisted. "I'm telling you, as soon as her car rolled up Miguel must have left."

"What were you talking about?" she demanded in a way that gave him no out.

Tyler sighed, bracing himself for the blowup. "Cards. We were talking about gambling."

"You are not teaching this boy to gamble." She practically shook with anger.

"Is that really what's important here?" he asked, but it was obvious she didn't care.

"I didn't bring him here to learn how to play cards."

"The boy is interested, Juliette. That's all."

"The boy," she snapped, her eyes shooting sparks, "is in need of good influences."

Tyler blinked, a little stunned at her viciousness. "You brought him here, Jules. I'm just doing what you needed me to do."

"No, what I need is for you to babysit this kid, not teach him how to gamble."

"I was just talking—"

"I don't want you to talk to him! I don't want you to look at him. If I had my way, he'd never have met you."

Her words echoed in the silence.

That he was surprised was stupid. That he was a little hurt was even more stupid. He knew what she thought of him, but her words had blown a hole through his chest.

He'd just been trying to help.

He took a step back and then another, the anger rolling off her just a little too painful.

"Tyler," she sighed, as if she was about to offer an apology she wasn't even close to meaning.

"No, no, of course. You wouldn't want me to rub off on your hoodlum. God forbid I teach him—" he shrugged "—what? Car theft?"

"No," she said. Her eyes narrowed and he knew she wasn't done. She had something she was dying to get off her chest. She stepped closer and the air sizzled and crackled, as though there was a stick of dynamite between them.

Here it comes, he thought. He should never have accused her of being cold.

Juliette was fire. She always had been.

"How to not give a shit about anyone but himself," she spat. "How to hurt people. How to walk away when someone cares about you, when someone has invested themselves in you."

He held up his hand, stopping her tirade. "I get it. You're scared I'm going to teach him to be like me."

She paused before nodding. That little nod, the play of light in her hair, in her eyes—the reflection and refraction, a world upon a world—destroyed him.

Juliette was close enough to smell, close enough to touch if he really wanted to watch her explode. And her standing there, thinking the worst of him, counting the minutes until he left made him want to lose his mind.

It made him want to ease her to the grass, take off those pants of hers. Feel those legs, endless and strong, wrap around his back. He wanted to cover her smart mouth with his. He wanted to lick her and bite her, feel her breath in his ear, her nails in his back. He wanted her under him, to remind her that even with all that smug superiority, bad, bad Tyler O'Neill could make good girl Juliette Tremblant want him so bad she'd scream with it.

Juliette stepped away, a blush on her cheeks, and Tyler guessed he didn't hide his desire very well.

"I need to go find Miguel," she said.

"You want help?" he asked, knowing the answer before he asked it.

She shook her head and Tyler nodded, feeling that if he opened his mouth there was no telling what would pour out.

He didn't watch her drive away. Instead he stepped up to the front door, now two feet above the ground with no porch.

Stupidly, it had never occurred to him that having torn

the damn thing down they'd have to rebuild it. And if this situation with Miguel was somehow over, he'd have to do the work himself.

Great. Just freaking great.

Once inside, his father crept out of the shadows, a bizarre housewife with a tumbler full of amber liquid at the ready. Tyler shook his head, waving off the glass.

"What do you say we drive over to Franklin Parish," Dad said. "Get ourselves some catfish and watch the dancing girls at Sully's."

Tyler didn't answer. He pulled his shirt over his head and draped it across one of the stools in the kitchen. His skin felt too tight, his head too full. The house was getting dark, night bleeding in moment by moment. Hours of time stretched in front of him with just his father for company.

I'm going to lose my mind.

"Son?"

"I'm going out," he said.

"Where?"

"Remy's." The old dance hall out in the bayou was exactly what he needed. Music. Beer. Beautiful women. And Remy. He wondered if Priscilla Ellis still worked the bar and he really, really hoped she did. He could use some kindness, a happy word in his ear.

"Good idea. Let me just get—"

"You're not coming," Tyler said.

JULIETTE FOUND MIGUEL pacing a hole in the carpet in Patricia's living room. She was barely through the door and into the shabby living room that smelled like laundry soap and cooking ground beef before he was charging down the hallway toward her.

"You said no social workers!" he yelled, anger making

him somehow younger and older at the same time. The big baggy sweatshirt he was wearing made him look like a babe in swaddling clothes.

"I didn't call them," she said, watching out of the corner of her eye as Patricia disappeared into the kitchen.

"Then who did?" he demanded and she shook her head. She'd been wondering the same thing, torn between Dr. Roberts and Ms. Jenkins at school. His face was still pretty messed up; the burn had faded, but not the worst of the bruises, and Ms. Jenkins might have finally had enough of Miguel's half truths and cover-ups.

But something in Juliette's gut said the surprise visit from the social worker had Owens's dirty fingerprints all over it. It was just a hunch, but it felt right.

"I don't know," she said, holding out her arms, wishing she could hug him and convince him that she would keep him safe.

But she couldn't lie, because the truth was, she might have screwed this up for everyone. Her mistakes might end up sending him into foster care.

Maybe her father was right. She was too soft for this job. Perhaps what she wanted to accomplish couldn't be accomplished from the Office of Police Chief.

She pulled her arms back to her sides, leaving them empty, the need to help an ache in her muscles. A burn in her fingers.

"But I am going to talk to the social worker and we'll get this all squared away, I promise."

"Yeah, you promised me shit before and it ain't worked out so well, has it?" he spat.

Louisa, his sister, crept out of the dark hallway to come stand by her brother. Her pretty black hair was pulled back in braids framing a round face, so sweet in its youth. In its innocence.

Juliette's heart cracked.

Louisa tucked her little hand in Miguel's and he held it, cradled it in his own not much bigger than hers. The two of them, two children, were a united front against a world determined to pull them apart.

"I'm not going to some foster home," he said. "We're not getting split up."

"I don't want you to get split up," she said, praying he would listen, that she could convince him, somehow, that after all this, she wanted him safe. "I don't want you to go to foster care. And right now, I'm telling you that your best shot of staying together is to wait this out. Let's see what happens with the social worker."

"I like you, Chief," he said.

"Me, too," Louisa piped up, and Juliette's throat burned with acidic regret.

"But I don't trust you," he said. "Not anymore. And I'm not going to sit at school waiting for you to show up with some woman who is going to take me away."

Hurt and regret, jagged pains right through her chest, made it impossible for her to speak and she wondered if this was how Tyler had felt tonight when she'd sliced him apart. She didn't think she could hurt him, didn't think he had feelings she could injure, but it was obvious she had.

She refused to feel guilty about what she'd said. She was just being honest and if Tyler was hurt by that, so be it.

But she had a bad feeling that Tyler was smack-dab in the middle of Miguel's situation whether Juliette liked it or not.

She swallowed her pride and it was bitter and hard, a rock in her chest. Sour in her heart.

"Do you…do you trust Tyler?" she asked, desperate.

Miguel shrugged and then, finally nodded. "I guess."

"Then whenever this meeting happens, I'll tell you and

you can stay with him," she said, and waited for Miguel to agree.

Miguel looked down at Louisa and stroked his little sister's hair, twined the long braid through his fingers.

"Miguel?" Louisa whispered. "What's happening?"

"Everything's going to be okay," he told his sister, and Juliette looked down through a haze at the worn nap of the red carpet, trying to keep her emotions schooled. Professional.

"Fine," he said. "We'll stay with Tyler."

She nodded, relief filling her with a cold wind.

But she knew she had to head back out to The Manor and make things right with Tyler. It killed her—destroyed her, actually—that after everything he'd done to her, the pain he'd inflicted, the doubt and confusion, she was going to have to apologize to him.

He'd torn her to the ground, ruined her. The person she'd become after he left was not the person she'd been before, and he'd done that to her.

But she needed him. Watching Miguel help his sister into her coat so Juliette could take them back to their crappy home, she needed Tyler more than ever.

And she hated it.

REMY'S WAS SO FAR OFF the beaten track you couldn't even find the road on a map. Tyler took Main out past the three oil drills and then took the first gravel road on his left. He followed that into the bayou, where the cypress and swamp crept closer and closer to the road. The gravel turned to dirt and twice Tyler had to stop because there was a big old croc in the middle of the road. Ten minutes out past the shack where the Louisiana State University bio students came out every spring to count dying plants, there was another dirt road that was actually Remy's long driveway.

The trees broke into a clearing, a strange little tongue of solid earth in the middle of the swamp, and Tyler parked Suzy beside the twenty or so other cars in the makeshift lot.

Remy's was alive tonight, every ragged Christmas light and Halloween decoration lit up, and it wasn't even eight. The smell of catfish and crayfish boil was so thick in the air Tyler could take a bite of it. And the music…the music pumped out the open windows and doors. Piano and guitar, an accordion and trumpet—bright riffs and solos, all of them calling him home.

Tyler pulled on his favorite blue linen shirt, buttoning the one button that was left over his white tank top, wondering if anyone in there would remember him. Remy would, but that might be all. There could be a room full of strangers, not a welcoming face among them.

"Is that Tyler O'Neill?" a woman cried, and Tyler smiled, recognizing the Marlboro-refined voice of Priscilla Ellis. He caught the glimmer and shine of her signature pink sequins out on the deck.

"Is that the most beautiful blonde in the state of Louisiana?" he asked, tucking his fedora on his head, tipping it over one eye.

Priscilla opened the door to the kitchen, a side door that spilled out onto the same wraparound front porch. "Remy!" she yelled. "Tell the band Tyler's here!"

He took the steps by threes and at the top he found himself in the ancient but unearthly strong grip of Priscilla's hug. Somewhere between sixty and a hundred, five foot nothing, a hundred pounds and as blonde as a bottle could make a woman—that was Priscilla. And she was perfect.

"Where you been, boy?" she asked, her black eyes sharp, her lips as pink as the sequined shirts she favored.

"Around," he answered, smiling down at her wrinkled face. This, he thought, more than The Manor, more than Bonne Terre, *this* was home. This woman and Remy and the stage in there, covered in cigarette butts and peanut shells.

"I wondered if you wouldn't come back around here after your momma's been poking her nose in places it don't belong."

He groaned—this was not why he'd come to Remy's. To talk about his reasons for being here, his mom. He wanted to play some jazz and forget.

"All right, I see you," Priscilla said. "But we're talking at some point, boy."

A giant Cajun man stepped out onto the porch, wiping his hands off on the apron around his thick waist. "I don't believe it," Remy said, his accent as thick as the swamp. "I just don't believe it."

"Hi, Remy." Tyler stuck out his hand but Remy pulled him in for a bone-crushing hug.

"You," Remy said. "You been gone too long." Tyler was surprised to see the big guy's eyes were wet. "That money you sent after Katrina—"

Priscilla crossed herself.

Tyler tried to stop the conversation before it got started. This gratitude business was always so damn uncomfortable. "Remy, seriously, you don't have to—"

"I do. I do have to thank you, and you have to listen. The boys in the band were able to feed their families and give them clothes and a place to stay until they got back on their feet. We got a few of them trailers for some folks around here."

"I'm glad," Tyler said.

"And this last bunch of money." Priscilla whistled. "Boy, you trying to buy the place?"

"No! No, I just know that times are tough and you guys know better than I do about people in these parts that need help the most."

"Well." Remy put his arm around Tyler, leading him in the back door through the steam and spice of the kitchen. Remy had to yell over the sounds of pots and pans and the cooks calling out Tyler's name. "People out here are grateful," Remy said while Tyler shook some hands. People he didn't know were thanking him for what he'd done for their families. "The band is waiting for you and tonight your money ain't no good. Now, what you need?" Remy asked, pounding Tyler on the shoulders.

"Let's start with a beer," Tyler said. His whole body, his heart and his head, the wounds from Juliette's disdain— everything was good. Healed. "And see where the night takes us."

JULIETTE PARKED HER SEDAN out front of The Manor. She killed the lights and the engine and sat there, in the dark, feeling every moment of her thirty-one years.

Resentment squeezed her throat tight, squashing the apology she was going to have to give Tyler.

She wasn't even sure if she could do this. Apologize. Ask him for more help, now adding Miguel's sister to the mix.

Laughter, surprised and exhausted, bubbled out of her chest. What a mess. What a freaking freak show of a mess. But sitting in her car doubting herself wasn't going to get anything done.

She threw open her door and stepped across the lawn to the bright red front door of The Manor.

Maybe he'd see the humor in this whole situation. He probably would. Everything was a joke to Tyler.

Maybe they could just have a laugh at how ridiculous all of this was and be done with it. Wouldn't that be nice?

The front porch was gone, and so she braced herself on the door frame and pulled herself up onto the narrow lip of the stoop.

The bright red door was cracked open.

Good Lord, didn't Tyler take anything seriously? She'd told him there had been suspicious activity, that his own mother had been caught breaking into the place because of some gems.

She pushed the door open and it squealed in protest.

"Miguel?" An older man who bore a remarkable resemblance to George Clooney stepped into the foyer and Juliette reached for her gun.

"Who the hell are you?" she demanded, and the man put his hands in the air, his eyes wide and blinking in shock.

"Richard," he said. "I'm Richard Bonavie—"

Juliette lowered the gun. The name rocketed out of the past and exploded in her chest.

"Tyler's father?" she whispered.

Ten years ago, Tyler had told her about Richard Bonavie; absent father and gambler. Ghost. And Tyler's voice had been bright with hero worship. Warm with all the love a parentless kid could create out of thin air.

Tyler found you, she thought, an errant pain and a wild pleasure zinging through her chest. *After all those years of dreaming about you, he finally found you.*

"Yes," Richard said, lowering hands. "I'm Tyler's dad. We're—"

"Why did you think I was Miguel?" she asked.

"Two nights ago he left his schoolbag. He came back that night." Richard lifted a backpack. "And he forgot it again today."

"Oh," she said, lowering her gun back to its holster.

Suddenly things didn't seem quite right. As the shock wore away the whole situation smelled slightly off.

"How long have you been here?" she asked.

"A week, maybe more," he said, with a casual shrug that Juliette saw through in an instant. A week? Tyler had gotten here on Sunday night. Why hadn't he told her that he was meeting his father here?

In fact…everything slowly, slowly clicked into place.

Oh, God, he'd lied. When she'd asked Tyler if there was anything suspicious or weird at The Manor, he'd said nothing. And maybe his father wasn't worth mentioning to Tyler, but it sure as hell was worth mentioning to her!

Why are you surprised? she wondered. She'd been waiting for something like this. Bracing herself for it. That she still managed to be shocked by Tyler's duplicity, by his total lack of ethics or even decency, was ridiculous.

She should know better.

"How much more?" she asked, her voice sharp, and Richard's smile got wider. Brighter. The confidence artist turning it up full blast.

"Not much."

"It was you," she said, connecting the dots, "that was sneaking around The Manor. The trampled plants, the damaged windowsills."

Richard laughed and Juliette stiffened. "I forgot my key and I was early," he said.

"You don't have a key," she snapped, ready to punish this man for Tyler's lies. "Margot and Savannah haven't seen or heard from you in years."

Suddenly she realized what this was all about.

"You're here because of the gems, aren't you?"

He blinked, feigning wide-eyed surprise. "Gems?"

She stepped up closer, tired of the games the O'Neill men seemed to love to run on her. "The gems aren't here," she said, silky smooth. "They never were. And if you're smart, you'll realize that and move on."

"I'm sorry, I'm confused. Is it a crime to spend time with my son? Have I done something wrong?"

Yes, she wanted to say. There's something really wrong about leaving your children to their evil bitch of a mother. And then staying away from your son, creating holes and gaps with your absence where misguided hero worship could grow like some kind of rotten vine.

"Maybe not," she said, but she would be running his name through the computer as soon as she had the chance. She'd bet good money that the man was wanted for something somewhere.

But right now she had bigger fish to fry.

"Where's Tyler?"

"Remy's," Richard said. "He left about an hour ago."

She reeled slightly at the name of the old jazz club, bombarded by a summer of memories she'd pushed away and tried to forget.

It was the last place she wanted to go, and Tyler was taking her back there, to the place where that summer had been most sweet.

And where the memories would be razor-sharp and waiting to slice her into ribbons.

CHAPTER NINE

JULIETTE STOOD IN REMY'S sand-and-gravel parking lot staring at the old shack, with its ridiculous lights and decorations. A grinning light up jack-o'-lantern from a Halloween party twenty years ago still blinked in a window.

She barely heard the music pouring through the broken screen door. All she heard was the pounding of her heart.

The dim echo of Tyler's words ten years ago.

You, his voice whispered from the past, making her stomach clench and her head spin, *you and a piano are all I want.*

"Right," she whispered, feeling herself begin to collapse, fold inward with the memories. And she couldn't have that.

He'd lied to her over and over again. About wanting her. Loving her. About his damn father being at the Manor.

She anchored herself in her hate, in her righteous anger, and she climbed the splintered wooden steps to the front door.

"Hold on a second there, sweetheart."

Pink sequins glittered in the darkness and Juliette felt a crushing mix of fondness and resignation.

Priscilla Ellis. Tyler's number-one fan. The old woman had never liked Juliette, which had more to do with Juliette's mother's money and her father's job. But to say the distrust went both ways was an understatement.

"You here to get that boy all worked up?" Priscilla asked, eyeing Juliette through a haze of smoke. "Run him off again?"

"I'm here to get some answers," Juliette replied, and Priscilla shook her head.

"I can't have that," Priscilla said. "That boy just came back and I need him."

"To play piano?" Juliette laughed, "Please—"

Priscilla appeared out of the shadows so fast Juliette took a step back. "You don't know Tyler," she said. "You never did. You overlooked everything about him you thought was bad, and only saw what you wanted. You picked him into pieces—"

"That's not true," Juliette breathed, alive with all she'd felt that summer. Every ounce of love turned back on her like a knife. "I loved him. I knew him—"

She stopped. She thought she'd known him. But then he'd left and everything she thought she'd known was destroyed.

"Just like you think you know him now," Priscilla said, taking a long drag on her Marlboro.

"I know what I need to," she said, through her teeth.

"Right," Priscilla said, taking her time with the word. "Tell me, you know about the money?"

"Don't tell me he stole money?"

"See, there you go," Priscilla said, the old woman getting angry. "You ain't no better than you were then. Wanting to believe the best, but unable to get away from the worst. He deserves better than you."

"He lied to me, Priscilla. You can stand there and be the authority on Tyler O'Neill, but he's lied to me at every turn."

Priscilla nodded. "He does do that," she said. "Hard to blame him, though. With no real momma—"

"Oh, stop," Juliette snapped. "Enough of the poor-Tyler-O'Neill story. Tell me about the money," she demanded, a shimmering feeling crawling up her back, telling her that her world was about to get knocked around again.

"You know Tyler sent that big check after Katrina?" Priscilla asked.

The floor rushed away from Juliette's feet. "No," she said, her voice firm.

"Remy bought those trailers outside of town with it, gave all those musicians and their families a place to stay."

Juliette couldn't have moved if she'd tried, and Priscilla just kept going, knocking down Juliette's version of Tyler like a punching bag.

"He sent another check just recently. We bought the land those trailers are on, and we're going to use the rest of the money to build permanent houses."

"Why do you need him here?" Juliette asked, her voice a whisper. "If you have the money, why do you need him?"

Priscilla shook her head as if disgusted by all that Juliette didn't know about Tyler.

But Juliette did know. Everything she'd learned about him that summer—that knowledge that she'd torched and buried—returned as a ghost, taunting her.

That boy who'd grown up without a mother, with only a false idol for a father. That boy who had more charm than shame, more heart than sense—that boy needed a home. And people to love him.

"Because he needs us," Priscilla said. "He needs to build those houses about as bad as we need them. And if you're going to ruin that, I'm going to have to ask you to leave, Chief."

Juliette was numb. Shaken.

"You going to ruin that?" Priscilla asked.

Maybe lying, she wasn't sure, Juliette shook her head and Priscilla watched her for another second before walking away.

I need to leave. I need to be far away from Tyler tonight.

But the pieces of herself—her skin, her heart and her aching sex—wanted to stay here. Wanted to find out the truth.

The screen door opened at her back and the heat and laughter and clink of glasses and plates flooded out, surrounding her with the sounds of the living.

The band started warming up again. The piano's big chords reverberated through Juliette's shell-shocked body. It was a wave, a current, and it swept her up and carried her inside.

The air tasted like spice and sweat. The band roared into their set and the dance floor was packed.

Through the bodies, she saw the band, and the world, her heart, every function of her body—stopped.

Sitting at the piano, a narrow fedora low over his eyes, a wrinkled linen shirt open over a damp white tank top was Tyler O'Neill. His fingers working the keys, his feet on the pedals, his whole body coiled and curled, pumping and shifting, working the piano as if it were a life-and-death race to some finish.

She didn't know how long she watched him, but Juliette was suddenly aware of her heart thundering in her chest, in her fingers, between her legs. Sweat beaded between her breasts, along her spine, and she felt like she had on too many clothes. There were simply too many things between her skin and the air that touched Tyler.

She felt everything she'd felt that summer when they came out here almost every night. Her, sick with love and lust, and Tyler, working up the nerve to play with the band.

They'd sit in the corner, his fingers on her leg under the table, or on her arm or back—playing her as if she were a keyboard.

"Go!" Tyler yelled, lifting his sweaty face to the thin black accordion player and they smiled at each other, sliding in and through some riff, some narrow and bright tunnel of music until finally the accordion player threw up his hands.

"I give, man, I give."

And then it was just Tyler.

He ran the back of his hands across the keys—a flourish—and stood up, the bench collapsing backward as if grateful for the break.

Remy's erupted into applause.

Tyler raised his arms and bowed back to the band, lifting a longneck from the floor and taking a long swig, the muscles of his neck flexing as he swallowed.

She felt flush watching him, hot and full. Ripe.

Miguel, Richard, Remy's, the music Tyler created—all of it turned to black and it was just Tyler.

Always Tyler.

TYLER TOOK THE BACK DOOR out into thick swamp, needing an escape from the gratitude and shameless women. Shameless women were usually his kind of woman, but tonight it felt all off. He was avoiding thinking about it too hard because he had a sinking suspicion that Juliette was at the root of that sudden and unfortunately timed change of heart.

The last time he'd been here had been with her, and he couldn't sit at that piano and not remember that. In fact, everywhere he looked he thought he saw her. The bright light of her eyes, the curve of her shoulder in a whisper thin shirt. Her hair, blue-black in the light.

But it was a trick. She would never come here. Never again, he'd made sure of that.

And ninety-nine percent of the time there wasn't a question in his mind that he'd done the right thing. That walking away from Juliette had been the best thing for her, of course with the added bonus of getting her father off his ass.

But tonight, he wished things were different. That he'd had a choice ten years ago that could have included her.

His shirt, soaked from neck to waist, stuck to him. He took it off, flinging the linen over his shoulder, and untucked his undershirt from the damp waistband of his old blue jeans. He'd forgotten what a workout Dixieland Jazz was.

The pier where Remy kept a few flat bottom fishing boats dipped under his weight, the water lapping quietly against aluminum and wood and whatever reptile was waiting for him to misstep and be dinner.

His lower back and wrists screamed from the abuse they were taking. Tomorrow he'd pay a fortune in aspirin for this good time, but he was just too damn content to care right now.

He couldn't remember the last time he'd felt this good. Maybe when he first got to Vegas. When he first found his dad and started winning some money. But then those good days just started to blend and the good became okay. And then they became bad.

And then it was just his life.

But this—friends, music, this wired and thrilling sense of joy—this wasn't anything he was used to. It was like remembering who he was—or who he had been.

Behind him, a shoe scuffed the worn wood and the pier dropped slightly under his feet.

A chill ran over his skin, a prickly awareness that told

him he wasn't alone. But then the scent of lemons cut through the mud-scented swamp air and he knew who was out here with him.

His eyes closed on a sigh.

"Go away," he said. He couldn't handle this. He was too raw tonight, too much himself to keep up all the bullshit, the lies he needed to tell her to keep the peace. "Please, just go."

I CAN'T, SHE THOUGHT. *God, I wish I could, but I am stuck here. With you.*

"I'll go," she said. "But I need a few answers."

"What have answers ever gotten you, Juliette?" he asked, his back still to her. His white undershirt stuck to him, hugging the muscles that her fingers and hands and lips remembered all too well.

She clenched her hands into fists. She was out here for a reason—she had purpose, and distraction would get her nowhere.

"Is what they're saying in there true?"

"Well," Tyler laughed and finally faced her. His blond hair was plastered to his forehead, but those blue eyes pulsed and glowed in the dark. He took a swig from the beer bottle in his hand. "If they're saying I'm the best piano player this side of Mississippi, then yes, I would have to admit—"

"Cut the bullshit, Tyler!" she cried, surprised and infuriated at the gaping cracks in her composure. "For once. Please. For me. Cut the crap."

He blinked and after a moment shrugged. "What do you want to know?" he asked before taking another drink, his eyes never leaving hers. She felt raw, naked under his gaze.

"Did you donate money to Remy after Katrina?"

Tyler licked his lips and nodded.

"And again, recently?"

"After I won the World Series thing," he said. "I know a lot of the folks around here, especially the musicians, don't have any savings."

"And you just happened to have a ton of cash."

"As a matter of fact—" His grin split the darkness like a knife and her breath hitched.

Unbelievably, tears scorched her eyes. She did not need this reminder of the man Tyler could be.

"Hey, hey," Tyler said, stepping up the pier toward her. "Don't get all worked up here. I'm still an asshole at heart."

His expression was that potent mix of boy and man and her composure cracked further. She winced under the power of her old love. Her old longings.

It wasn't enough that he'd left her, but he'd taken a huge part of her with him. For any man but this one—this blue-eyed devil in worn jeans and cowboy boots—she was stone-cold.

"I met your father tonight," she said, her voice a knife she jabbed at his chest. He winced and swore. "I went to your house to talk to you about Miguel, and you can imagine my surprise when your father answers the door."

Tyler winced. "He's harmless."

"Then why didn't you tell me? Why did you lie?"

"Because he's my dad!" he cried, as if it were that simple. And maybe for Tyler it was, and that was the problem. Tyler's loyalties were those of a ten-year-old boy. "Look, full disclosure. His roommates in Los Angeles were arrested for credit-card fraud—"

"You are kidding me!"

"Dad was questioned and released. He had nothing to do with it."

"So why is he here?"

"He just needs a place to stay."

"And you're suddenly the soul of generosity? Taking care of the homeless and your father and a beat-up kid?" She was spinning closer and closer to the edge of a question, a cliff she swore she'd never approach—but she couldn't stop herself. Her every defense was in ruins. Every lie she'd told herself about Tyler O'Neill had been ripped from her, leaving her empty and cold.

"Is this more of the Tyler O'Neill sleight of hand?" she asked. "The guessing game? Which part is the real you and which part is the bluff? Which part is the guy handing out money to the poor and which part is the man who walked away—" Her voice cracked and she stopped, grasping with everything in her for control.

"Whatever it's easiest for you to believe, Juliette. Go with that. Don't break your head trying to figure me out."

"It's a little late for that, Tyler! Or did I imagine that summer? Did I make that up? You and me and the Chevy and coming out here every night. Did I make up your kisses and the way you touched me? Those things you told me about moving to New Orleans and how we'd live in the French Quarter and you'd play the piano and I'd get my law degree? Was that real? Did I make that up?"

"No." He was so still. So quiet. "It was real."

"Then why did you go?"

The words tumbled out, words she'd wondered a million times, and now, now that he was here and her heart was pumping out fresh hurt, they were unstoppable.

Tyler froze as if the question had a power over him he couldn't fight.

"Don't," he breathed, "do this to yourself."

She laughed, the sound vicious and hard, and he closed

the last distance between them. He was so close she could smell him, taste the spice of him on her tongue. A buzz filled her head, a warning that she was too close. Too close to him and too close to doing something stupid.

"Juliette," Tyler breathed, his eyes roving over her face like fingers over Braille, "I'm not worth whatever it is you're doing to yourself."

"Then tell me why you left!" she snapped, and he flinched. "What did you think would happen when I woke up that morning and realized you'd left me, left me after I'd lied to my father for months, after I'd slept with you and given you every single part of myself, after I'd told you that I loved you? Did you think I wouldn't notice? Or that I wouldn't care that you left without a word!" She was screaming. "Not one word, Tyler!"

"I know," he whispered. "I do, I know."

She slapped him. Because he *didn't* know. He had no goddamned idea of the pain she'd lived with.

Her hand burned and the buzz in her head turned to a roar.

Tyler's jaw clenched and his eyes blazed and for a second she wondered if he might slap her back. She would welcome it. She would welcome the chance to totally kick his ass.

"Feel better?" he asked, his cheek turning red.

"No."

"Me, neither," he said.

And then he kissed her. His mouth hard against hers, a slap in kiss form. Craving something violent, she grabbed his shirt and pulled him to her. Her mouth opened and she devoured him, would have swallowed him whole if she could. If she could just get close enough.

He groaned and wrapped his arms around her, low

around her hips, and lifted her against him, notching her against his erection.

His flavor exploded in her. His heat and scent pummeled her. She fisted her hands into his hair, raking the skin of his shoulders with her nails and he groaned low in his chest. A growl of desire and want and need that her entire body echoed.

"There's not been one day I have not thought of you," he said and it took a moment for his words to register. To slide cool fingers down her spine, extinguishing the fire in her belly.

"What?" she breathed. Her body was slow to follow her brain's directions, but she let go of him. She pushed away, letting the night in between them.

Tyler's blue eyes were unreadable and she wanted to smack him again. "You can't just say that, Tyler. You can't—"

"Forget it, Juliette," he said, and it was as if a light went out in him. "Forget about me. I was never worth what you gave me."

He stepped past her, back up the pier and the party going on inside. The door opened and someone yelled his name and Tyler laughed, the sound like being blasted by glass and she gasped for breath.

"On my way!" he yelled, Tyler the piano man reborn, and then he was gone.

A PEANUT SHELL, SANDWICHED between the piano bench and Tyler, was digging its sharp little claws into Tyler's shoulder blade. It hurt. A lot, actually. But what did a guy expect trying to sleep on a piano bench?

With a peanut shell and a hangover the size of the Gulf for company.

He ignored the discomfort for as long as he could, trying

to find a comfortable place on the hard bench while his head pounded and his back muscles burned.

It didn't take a genius to figure out what had happened to his night. Even though the last thing he remembered was walking away from Juliette, his head told him he'd drowned the taste of that kiss in some bourbon and his back told him he'd pounded out his frustration on the piano.

Not that it had worked—he was still frustrated and the taste of that kiss remained on his tongue.

But there was something delicious happening in the air, and his stomach growled. Coffee. Bacon. Unfiltered Marlboros.

There were worse places to wake up hungover and sore than Remy's.

"Wake up, Tyler." Someone poked at his leg and he nearly lost his precarious bed.

Gingerly, he sat up, and peanut shells popped off his back like hard bog leeches.

"Morning, Priscilla," he groaned. Blindly he held out his hand and a warm ceramic mug was pressed into it. The sweet smell of Remy's chicory coffee made divine with about eight tablespoons of sugar was almost enough to coax his eyes open. Almost.

"You were a man on fire last night," Priscilla said. "That last set." She whistled long and low.

Priscilla's whistles were a language of their own. This whistle was loaded and he knew she didn't want to talk about music. This whistle had "let's talk about your sad life" all over it.

He grunted.

"Sure brings back memories," Priscilla went on, about as subtle as a water buffalo in a tutu. "'Course, you spending the night here reminds me of a few years ago, too."

"If you have a point," he muttered, "go ahead and get to it."

"Not worth it if you're gonna sit there half-dead."

He blinked open his eyes, his retinas screaming at sunshine's kamikaze assault.

"I didn't know this place had windows," he muttered.

It took a while, but he glanced around surprised at how clean the place was. Spotless except for the little island of peanut shells and beer bottles around him.

Priscilla sat on a chair in front of the stage, wrapped in a subdued pale yellow robe. In the bright sunlight she almost looked her age—not that he could tell what that was.

"What are you doing back here?" she asked.

"A boy can't visit his family?"

"The whole parish knows The Manor is sitting empty these days. There's no family of yours to visit right now."

"I can't come visit you and Remy?"

"'Course you can. But you're not here for us." She narrowed her eyes. "I got a bad feeling it has something to do with the rumor your momma was in town not long ago, looking for some gems."

Tyler smiled and stared into his mug, seeing his reflection in the black.

"There are no gems," he said. "There probably never were. I've searched that house inside and out."

"What about your momma? You telling me her being around wasn't a draw?"

"That was part of it," he said, sitting in a pool of sunshine, thoughts of his mother just floated through him instead of weighing him down.

He sucked down the coffee and shuddered as it jackknifed into his system.

"What you planning, boy?"

"The Spanish Inquisition?" he joked, but just barely. Somewhere in the back of his mind he had a bunch of things he wanted to say to his mother. He wanted answers to questions that kept him up nights. But he knew in his heart of hearts that it was fruitless. The questions about why she'd left him, Savannah and Carter and how she'd left them would go unanswered, and frankly, it was about time he moved on. Stopped being a kid left on a doorstep by a mother who didn't care about him.

"Truth is," he said, unsure of why he was even talking about this. But that's what booze and music and kissing the best woman he'd ever known got him—confused, weak. "I was lonely."

"You?" Priscilla asked with a snort. "What about that girlfriend of yours? That French woman."

"It didn't work out." He left it at that, the whole story too depressing to get into with the feel of Juliette branded back into the skin of his arms like a graft from the past.

"Well, I'm not sure what you expect," Priscilla said, taking a sip of coffee. "You live in Las Vegas. In a hotel. I've never heard of anything so lonely in my life."

"It seemed like a good idea at the time," he said, as though the past ten years of his life could be considered "a time."

"Well, you're here now," she said, as if him being here meant something. And because he was weak and the feel of Juliette's skin was burned into his flesh, he wanted it to mean something.

He wanted to be here because this was his home.

Priscilla sat there, a hundred pounds of speculation and anticipation, and Tyler just didn't have the strength to wait her out.

"Okay, just say it," he said.

"She was here," Priscilla said, and Tyler stared down

at his cup instead of answering. She. Despite the women in his family, there was only one *she* in his life around here.

"You got a death wish over that woman?" Priscilla asked.

Tyler sighed. "I think so, yes."

"It's not funny. She's police chief over in Bonne Terre."

"That's what I'm told," he drawled.

"I would have thought that ten years ago you might have learned your lesson. A woman like that, she's just—"

Tyler held up his hand. After tasting Juliette's anger and rage—her never-ending hurt—things were unclear in his head. He thought she'd get over him in time. That after a few months away from him, a couple of handsome men to take her mind off her broken heart, she'd move on.

The anger wasn't surprising. She deserved to be angry.

But the pain...the pain was still so real. So fresh. Like seeing him ripped a bandage off a wound that wasn't healed.

That he felt the same way made it all so much worse. Looking at her, seeing her, kissing her again last night— dumb move. Very dumb move. He'd blame the night and the music, hell, he'd blame it on swamp gas.

But even if it killed him, he had to try to make it right with her. Come clean about his father. About the past.

I'm going to have to apologize, he realized, not much liking the idea.

"Trust me, I learned my lesson," he said, trying to end the conversation.

"So what was last night?"

He sighed, tipping his head back, wishing there was some kind of answer to that question that made sense,

that wasn't locked up in the past and those old feelings for
Juliette.

I love her, he thought but could never say. *I always
have.*

"I have no idea."

Priscilla's eyes snapped and she uncrossed her legs,
leaning forward, all but breathing fire.

"Then stay away, Tyler. Women like her…" She trailed
off, and maybe it was the hangover or the peanut shell, but
whatever it was, he was pissed.

"Women like her what?"

"She's not for you."

Tyler nodded, his temper a bear coming out of hiberna-
tion. *The likes of us.* He'd been hearing that crap his whole
damn life.

"What does that mean, exactly?" he asked, his voice
cutting through the haze of Priscilla's cigarette. "Because
I'm rich now, Priscilla. I mean, I've got way more money
than the Tremblants ever did."

"It's not about money. It's about blood. It's about what
people think."

"Well, it's not like Jasper Tremblant has been a model
citizen his whole life," he said, thinking about the night
he left and Jasper's role in the whole thing. "I don't see
him pumping huge amounts of money back into his community."

He felt slimy tooting his own horn like that, but sometimes being the unsung hero got a little old, particularly
when everyone around here still thought he was white
trash.

"You're right, that man's got some wires crossed, that's
for sure. But I'm just saying—out in the world, you can be
whoever you want. But here—" she arched her thin eye-

brows "—you're a Notorious O'Neill. The worst of them. And that's all that woman is ever gonna see."

Tyler swallowed his anger. He was too tired to hold on to a fight.

But Priscilla is wrong, a voice in his head said. *You can be different. And Juliette always knew that about you.*

"Well, since you're here, we could use you," she said.

"I can come out on weekends," he said. "Play with the band."

"That ain't what I'm talking about. We need your help building them houses."

"Oh, come on now, Priscilla, we both know that's not me."

"Why? 'Cause it's honest work?" she asked.

"No," he said. "Because I don't know the first thing about building anything." And frankly, the idea was ridiculous. His hands were baby soft, not a callous on them. And he liked it that way.

He cocked his head, turning those words over in his head. Words that could have come right out of his father's mouth.

You don't want to be like him, he thought. *Now is your chance. Prove you're more than a Notorious O'Neill. Prove you're better.*

"We don't know much, either," Priscilla said, and then dropped her voice to a whisper. "Remy's about useless with a hammer. Swear, he's gonna put himself in the hospital before something actually gets to standin'."

"So?" Tyler asked. "Who's really doing the build?"

"People in town. Derek at the hardware store has a crew. You could go and talk to him."

Priscilla stood and her palm, soft and frail, the skin like silk and paper, landed against his cheek. "You need to find a woman who sees the real you," she said. "Sees past that Notorious O'Neill stuff."

Maybe it was the girls he chose or maybe it was just him—but no one ever saw past what he showed them.

Except Juliette.

"Hey, now." She stepped back, affronted. "You like being alone, Ty?"

He thought about saying yes, that he was happy this way. But that nightmare with Theresa, the way he let his father hang around like bad fish, the way he felt when he saw Juliette—like seeing the world in color after years of black-and-white—he couldn't actually get the lie out of his mouth.

And suddenly, he felt more alone than he could bear.

"Oh, honey," she sighed, his silence answer enough for both of them. "You deserve better. You're not your father."

"You know, one minute she's not for me and the next minute I'm too good for her. Which is it, Priscilla?" he asked. "Am I a good man or am I a Notorious O'Neill?"

Priscilla lit up another smoke. "That," she said with a cagey smile, "is a very good question."

It took a moment, but then he shook his head—she'd gotten him again. But he was too far gone to psychoanalyze himself right now.

"I need to go," he said, the specter of what his father—no doubt bored and feeling neglected—might be up to haunting him.

But then Remy walked in from the kitchen with three plates piled high with eggs and bacon.

"Sit yourselves down," Remy said, sliding the heavy

plates on the table. "I got pecan bread coming out of the oven."

"On second thought," he said, his stomach growling. "I can stick around for a little while."

CHAPTER TEN

MONDAY, FIVE IN THE AFTERNOON, and Juliette was ice-cold. Unmovable. She was a glacier of cold purpose, and Tyler O'Neill—the kiss, the night out at Remy's, the truth about those houses and the money he'd given back to the town—were nothing to her.

She glanced in her side view mirror and could just see Tyler's head, his blond hair glinting white in the sunlight. He and Miguel were working on something, their heads bent together for the past ten minutes.

She put on her mirrored aviator glasses and stepped out of her sedan into the humidity of the September afternoon.

Ready to face down Tyler O'Neill.

The grass crunched under her boots and she gathered great strength from imagining it being Tyler's testicles.

"Miguel," she said as she approached, the sharpness in her voice surprising even her. Both Miguel and Tyler jumped as if she'd fired her weapon at them.

Not a great start, but she didn't apologize, not even when Miguel blew out a shaky breath and tried to laugh. "Wow, Chief," he said. "You about killed me."

"You ready to go?" she asked. She hated the sound of her voice, all the hard and brittle edges, barely camouflaging her feelings about Tyler more than if she just threw herself on the grass and cried.

Not as cool as she wanted to be. At all.

"Sure," Miguel said, shooting Tyler a puzzled glance. "Let me get my stuff."

As soon as he left, Juliette's skin shrank a size and she was painfully aware that she was alone with Tyler. And that he was staring at her. "I need a favor," she said, watching him through her sunglasses, grateful for the barrier. "I have an appointment with Nora Sullivan from the Office of Community Services—"

"I remember Nora," he said, and shuddered. She forced herself not to smile, because Nora's demeanor was chilly to say the least.

"It's Wednesday morning. Can you keep an eye on Miguel and his sister?"

"Isn't it a school day?" he asked.

Juliette nodded. "I need to know where he is, and he'll skip if he knows I'm meeting with Nora that day."

"So don't tell him."

"I promised him I would. And frankly, I've broken a lot of promises to Miguel. I don't want to break this one."

Tyler's gaze was a warm weight, comforting, and she didn't want to be comforted. Not by him. "Will you do it?" she demanded, sounding like a bully. Like her father.

Tyler sighed, looking out over The Manor, not answering.

"You want me to beg?" she asked.

"Of course not," he said, "but I don't think I deserve to be treated this way."

He was right, which gave her a moment of hot shame, but then she was only further pissed off. Like she needed a lesson in manners from him.

"Please," she said. "Can you help me?"

"Of course." He was so reasonable, calm, which made her feel even smaller and more petty. Nervous. Terrified of what would happen if she let go of all her anger, the years of cold comfort her hate had brought her.

"Thanks," she said, sounding about as gracious as a rock. He continued to watch her, and the ghosts of the past, the pains and pleasures, suddenly haunted the air around them.

"Juliette," he said, his voice soft and much closer than it should be.

"Don't," she whispered, and stepped away, sensing something awful on the tip of his tongue. Something that would change how she felt about him. How she dealt with him. "Don't do this—"

"Juliette, I'm sorry."

For the kiss, she thought, and she almost laughed. Almost screamed, actually, because she was a total mess and he tore down all her walls, ran through all her doors.

"I'm sorry for the way I left," he said. "Ten years ago."

Her head went light and she was dizzy. *Now he apologizes?* she thought, feeling shaky and furious. Her knees trembled, weakened, but she locked them. The urge to look at him, to lift her glasses and stare point-blank into his eyes and read his regret like a book, was so powerful she had to clench her hands into fists to keep herself from doing it.

Instead, she stared at a honeybee's slow climb over a blade of grass.

"I was a kid and I was scared. I was…terrified, actually, because you were going to give up Oklahoma State, for me. For us. And I knew I wasn't worth you doing that. I wasn't worth any of what you gave me."

Her mind was a vacuum, an empty wasteland of bitter memory. A stinging melancholy filled her, pushing aside her anger.

"Jules," he breathed. "Please say something."

Finally she looked at him, her hungry eyes seeing all of his contrition and anxiety. He needed her to accept this apology, she realized, far more than she needed to hear it.

Which surprised her and made her only more sad that they were who they were to each other.

"Am I supposed to forgive you now?" she asked, her voice shaken. "You apologize, I say no problem and…what? We're friends? Or maybe…more?"

"I have no motives, Juliette."

"*Please,*" she nearly howled. "Tyler O'Neill with no motives. Who are you kidding?"

His lips were tight, white in the corners, and she relished those small signs of his distress.

"Fine." She shrugged. What did it matter in the end—apology or not, their future was nonexistent. Putting the past to bed made no difference. "Your apology is accepted."

"You're lying," he said. "You don't forgive me at all—"

"You're not asking for forgiveness," she said. "And you're right. I don't forgive you. But I accept your apology, because it doesn't change anything, Tyler. Just like the kiss. Nothing is different. You're still you."

"Notorious O'Neill," he spat, and she nodded.

"The worst of them."

His eyes narrowed. Hardened. "And you're still you," he said, leaning closer, his breath fanning her face, the smell of him going right to her knees. Her head. Her stupid heart.

"And I've got your number," he whispered. "You want to pretend that kiss meant nothing, fine. It was nothing. But I'm not the one who walked in here with a favor and mirrored sunglasses and a chip on her shoulder, so if you want to pretend that nothing's different, feel free. But I'm not buying it, Jules. I'm on to you."

His anger struck hers and shot sparks all over the yard. She couldn't breathe for the tension between them. The sudden wild temptation to crush her lips to his and take out this fury on him.

"It doesn't have to be this hard, Jules," he said, his eyes on her lips, the pounding of her heart in her throat. "I can be your dirty little secret again."

Miguel cleared the corner.

Oh, thank God.

She turned around and headed for the car, the taste of blood in her mouth from where she'd bitten her lip.

"Let's go," she said to Miguel, not looking at Tyler, putting as much distance as she could between them. Between her and the apology she'd been waiting ten years for. And the truth that he'd seen in her, despite her efforts to hide it all.

Her hands shaking, she pulled open the door of her car.

A few moments later, Miguel slid in beside her and a shadow fell over her face. She knew without looking that Tyler stood beside her car, blocking out the sun, taunting her because he could.

"You okay?" Miguel asked.

"Just great," she said. She lifted her glasses to the top of her head and turned to look at Tyler, gilded with sunshine and charm, a beautiful, faithless Apollo sent to ruin her life. Again.

He's helping you, some unwanted sensible voice pointed out. *He's doing what you couldn't ask anyone else in this town to do, so how about you drop the bitch routine and act like a decent person?*

She didn't want to be sensible. She didn't want to be forgiving or humble. The high road had no interest for her, because she had the terrible feeling that accepting this apology might lead to forgiving him, which might lead to spending time with him. Which might lead places she had no business going.

Nope, she'd keep her anger and stick to the low road. Where she was safer.

WEDNESDAY MORNING, JULIETTE dropped the kids off with Tyler at the Sunrise Breakfast counter for scrambled eggs and milk shakes.

At eight in the morning.

Only Tyler, she thought, torn between exasperation and uncomfortable fondness.

I can be your dirty little secret again.

His words lived on in her body, stoking fires that had long been cold.

And it would be driving her out of her mind if Juliette didn't have much bigger problems to deal with.

She had Nora Sullivan and the potential destruction of her career to worry about.

At some point during her sleepless night she had made up her mind that she wasn't going to make anything difficult for Nora, she was just going to rip the bandage, as it were, right off, instead of pulling it back one careful, painful piece at a time.

And maybe today she'd get some kind of sign, an answer about her doubts that she was right for this job.

But twenty minutes later when Nora Sullivan walked in Juliette's office, Juliette had a brief panic. In a glance, she knew why Miguel ran. Hell, Juliette felt like running. Nora looked like the kind of woman who knew how to give bad news and didn't mind doing it.

Unbelievably, the woman wore a pink silky shirt with a little lace at the neck. She was like a bulldog with a ruffled collar.

"Nora," Juliette said, standing up at her desk to shake the woman's hand, trying her damndest to get this meeting off on even footing. "Thanks for coming in."

"It's my job," Nora said, and sat in the chair opposite Juliette's desk. Nora wasted no time before taking a file from her briefcase and moving Juliette's nameplate and her academy mug filled with pens and highlighters to the side.

Make yourself at home, Juliette thought, trying to keep her cool while Nora opened the file.

"You're younger than I expected," Nora said.

Juliette had heard that a lot, but now she wondered for the first time if it was a problem. "I worked harder than most to get here," she said. "My age has not affected my work."

Nora pursed her lips. "Well, it certainly explains some of the mistakes you've made with Miguel." She bent back to her file while Juliette seethed with embarrassment and self-consciousness. "We got a call—"

"From whom?" Juliette asked.

Nora glanced at Juliette through thin blond eyelashes. "That's confidential."

Juliette knew that, but hearing about that anonymous tip sparked her anger and she sat in her chair, surrounded by the portraits of the chiefs that came before her, including her father, and fumed.

"Nora, I was hoping we could make this as easy as possible—"

Nora sat back. "You were?" she asked. "Your actions previous to this meeting would suggest a total unwillingness to make this process easier."

Juliette's stomach dropped into her knees.

It's going to be like that, is it?

"We've started the investigation process and opened a file on Miguel Pastor and his sister," Nora continued. "According to school records, Miguel's had some truancy issues. Nothing too alarming and his grades are good. His sister—"

Juliette held up her hand. "I'll tell you what I know," she said, and she grabbed the edge of that Band-Aid and ripped.

She told Nora about Miguel's trying to steal the car, how Tyler didn't press charges. About the informal community service and finally about Miguel's father. The abuse.

"Are there medical records substantiating the abuse?"

Juliette shook her head. "He lied, and I let him," she said, meeting Nora's disapproving eyes. "We knew the doctors would call the office of community services and Miguel was adamant about not going to foster care. He worried about he and his sister getting split up—"

"He ran when he saw me that day at the O'Neill house."

"I found him. I mean, I've never been worried about where to find him," Juliette said, each word sounding like a lame excuse. A tired reason. Every single thing she thought had been right, was now, clearly, so damn wrong. "But I was worried about what kind of trouble would have found him first."

Nora nodded and sat back in her chair, the soft morning sunlight softening her face, but not her eyes. Her eyes were double-barreled shotguns, pointing right at Juliette.

"You realize as an officer of the law you are a mandated reporter of child abuse."

"I...do. Yes."

"Had the abuse been more serious, you could lose your job."

Juliette nodded. "I understood the risks I was taking."

Nora snorted and crossed her arms over her chest.

"You know what galls me?" Nora asked. "What really worries me about this situation? You let a scared sixteen-year-old boy dictate your actions."

"I was trying to keep him out of Department of Corrections. We don't have programs or services in place to help kids," Juliette said.

"The Parish does," Nora said. "I am a part of a program designed to help kids. I understand that he was scared. And I agree—he was a flight risk. But you are the adult, and you didn't do your job."

Juliette nodded, shamed into silence that buzzed painfully in her ears.

"What happens now?" she finally asked.

"I'm going to visit Ramon Pastor and let him know that community services has opened a file on Miguel and Louisa. And that should there be any more instances of abuse or attempted crime, we'll remove the child from his home. We'll enroll the family in counseling—"

"Ramon won't go," Juliette said.

"You don't know that," Nora said, her thin lips tight. "And frankly, your assumptions have led us to this mess. But if Miguel's father does not make efforts to keep his children, then we will find foster homes for the kids."

Juliette groaned. "He'll die without his sister. I'm telling you, Miguel is a good kid, a sweet kid who is trying hard to stay that way, but you take his sister away and pretty soon he'll end up in DOC because he deserves to."

Nora nodded in stern sympathy. "Sadly, there are problems that arise, but with a good community support—"

"We don't have community support," Juliette said,

feeling her face get hot with panic. "That's what I'm trying to say. We have no system in place to help a kid like Miguel."

"It seems to me you do," Nora said, looking down at her file. "Tyler O'Neill. Trust me, systems in other towns all started with a citizen like Mr. O'Neill—someone who has the time, energy and inclination to help. You can grow your own system, Chief Tremblant."

With Tyler as the seed? It was the most ridiculous thing she'd ever heard. Giving money to down-and-out musicians and funding the cost for new homes was not the same as an outreach program for at-risk kids.

Unwanted, the thought of his face sitting at that breakfast counter between Louisa and Miguel seared her brain.

Sure, she thought bitterly, *he could do it. Kids like him. Trust him. But would he do it? For extended periods of time?* The answer resounding emphatically through her body was no.

"Another place to start is in your own department," Nora said. "Designate one of your employees to be a family officer, to act as a liaison between myself and—"

"I'll do that," she said quickly.

"That's good." Nora slid a card across the desk toward Juliette. "As chief, that sends a powerful message to the community that you're involved."

Something bright bubbled in Juliette's chest, a potent mix of hope and satisfaction.

This was good, she realized. This was how she was going to be police chief her way.

"Contact Officer Rhodes in Ellicott City. He's the family officer there and he has an excellent system in place. He was in the same bind you are in a few years ago."

Juliette stared down at the card and decided to take the

bulls by the horn. "Will there be some kind of action taken against me for not reporting the abuse?"

"I have to put a letter of reprimand in your file. But I'll decide what else needs to be done after I talk to Miguel." She began to pack up her briefcase, every movement efficient and clipped. "He's not at school today. Neither is his sister." She arched her light eyebrows. "I am assuming you know where we can find them?"

Juliette nodded and stood, numb to the anxiety and worry. To the strange embarrassment of having been proven not so clever after all.

"I'll drive," she said.

"TYLER," MIGUEL SAID, his voice conveying a world of skepticism that frankly, Tyler was not appreciating. They were carrying the lumber from his new truck to the soon-to-be-rebuilt-better-than-ever porch. Tyler kept glancing over his shoulder to make sure Louisa was coming with the boxes of nails.

So cute, that kid.

"Where's your enthusiasm?" he asked, sliding his two-by-twelves onto the grass.

Miguel just stared back at him blankly.

"Come on, it'll work," Tyler said, pulling the plans he'd sketched up last night from his back pocket. He unfolded the piece of paper, tried to smooth out the worst of the wrinkles and, after stealing some masking tape stuck to one of the bundles of boards, taped them to the front of the red door. "Won't it, Louisa?"

"Yep," she said, putting the boxes of nails next to the boards.

"But have you ever built anything like this?" Miguel asked.

"No," Tyler said.

"You ever designed—"

"This is my first," Tyler said.

"This ain't ever going to work," Miguel said.

"Your lack of faith is truly insulting," Tyler said.

"My lack of faith?" Miguel scoffed. "Dude, you been sitting in a chair refusing to help me tear down a porch because you said you got no clue how to do it. Now, you draw up some crap on a—" Miguel flicked the paper on the door, glancing at the back of it "—flyer for a strip club? And you think I'm going to be able to build it? A porch? By myself?"

"First of all," Tyler said. "Sully's is not a strip club. It's a gentleman's club and someday you will understand the difference." Tyler stepped over to the piles of lumber and grabbed the two tool belts. He pretended to hand one to Miguel, but at the last minute he handed it to Louisa, who howled with laughter.

He needed to keep this girl around all the time; she was great for his ego.

"And second, I don't expect you to build it. I expect us to build it," Tyler said.

"Me, too?" Louisa asked.

"Of course. Who else will be using all the power tools?"

"She's not touching any power tools!" Miguel cried, his voice climbing ten octaves.

"It's a joke, kid." Tyler smiled at the boy's steamed expression. "You've got to lighten up. Derek helped me with the plans and told me what kind of lumber and tools we needed. He measured and cut most of the wood."

"Derek gonna come over here and help us build it?"

"No. Come on, man. You and I can do this."

Miguel squinted at him, sizing him up. The boy's face was getting better; he still looked like he'd been roughed up, but the burn was less vivid and the bruising was turning yellow.

"First you buy that crappy truck—"

"Don't call Lila crappy," Tyler said. "She's sensitive about her age."

"Now you're building porches?" Miguel shook his head. "I always knew you were strange, but this is a whole new level of weird. You're changing and it ain't pretty."

Changing, Tyler thought. *I can only hope.*

"Hey, Miguel?" Louisa said, her voice suddenly smaller than Tyler had heard it all day. "Who is that with Juliette?" she asked, sidling up next to Tyler, reaching for Miguel's hand.

Miguel and Tyler turned to see Juliette crossing the lawn with Nora Sullivan.

Shit.

"Miguel!" Juliette cried. "We just want to talk."

"Louisa, come on," Miguel whispered, backpedaling past the porch. "Run."

CHAPTER ELEVEN

"WHOA!" TYLER SAID, AND HE scooped up Louisa, stopping Miguel in his tracks.

"Let her go," Miguel breathed and Tyler held Louisa closer. "Come on, man. You know that woman is going to take us away."

Louisa pressed her face into his shirt, sounds like a kicked dog coming out of her throat.

"You're scaring her," Miguel snapped.

"No, Miguel, you are. Listen to me." Tyler tried to loosen Louisa's firm grip on his windpipe. "You can run, but…but sometimes it's smarter to see what you're running from."

The words were barely out his mouth before Juliette was there and Tyler realized how terribly ironic it was that he should say that. He'd run away from the best thing that had ever happened to him. He'd known that, and still he'd run.

"Miguel," Juliette said. "Ms. Sullivan just wants to talk to you. She's not taking anyone anywhere."

She reached for Miguel but he stepped away and Nora Sullivan took over like an arctic wind. "We need to talk, Miguel," she said, and Miguel froze. Even Louisa stopped whimpering. "As the person taking care of Louisa, you need to be making some smart decisions, and running away with her, with no money and no means to get anywhere, isn't a smart decision."

Miguel blinked and Tyler had to hand it to Nora. Treating the boy like an adult held him spellbound.

"Louisa?" Nora asked with a smile that softened her face. "Could you come and talk to your brother and I for a moment?"

Louisa loosened her death grip on Tyler's throat and took the few steps between Tyler and her brother.

"If you'd give us a moment?" Nora said, dismissing Tyler and Juliette, and they both nodded, easing around to the other side of the porch.

Once out of sight, Juliette turned away from him, braced her hands on her hips and took deep breaths, staring up at the sky, calming some panic inside her.

"Juliette—"

There was a second during which Tyler felt his heart beating in his face, his hands, his feet.

He'd sworn after that botched apology that he was going to let go of Juliette. In his mind. His heart. He was going to just let this end because he couldn't stand it anymore. Loving her and being hated by her tore the skin from his bones.

But he couldn't watch her in pain and not feel it.

Finally she turned with a slicing smile and over-bright eyes that didn't fool him for a minute.

"Oh, Jules—" He reached for her but she lifted her hand, her eyes blazing, and he stopped, the motion unfulfilled.

"Everything okay?" he asked.

"I have no clue," she said, jerking her shoulders. "No idea. I won't lose my job, but that hardly matters if those two get split up."

"You've done everything you can," he said.

"Really? Because right now, it seems all I've done is broken the law, several times. Kept Miguel and his sister in a dangerous home environment, trusted them to your keeping…"

He backed up. This again. He shouldn't have baited her the other day. That dirty little secret thing had just made things worse and he didn't want that. They were on the same team when it came to those kids and he just kept antagonizing Juliette.

Not that she didn't deserve it, but still. He was trying to be a better man.

"I'm sorry," she whispered. "You don't deserve that. You've been…great. Better than—"

"You could expect?" He smiled to make it a joke but she wasn't laughing.

"Better than anyone else would have been. And more important, you stepped in, when no one else would."

"I was just trying to get into your pants," he said with a shrug. "Hasn't worked."

Her laugh sounded like it was escaping a choke hold and then, suddenly, it was that laugh of hers he remembered. Like standing under a cool shower on a hot day.

Danger, he thought, but he couldn't back away if he had to. Juliette laughing. She was no longer the cold stranger; she was the girl he loved—the girl who had loved him. Her laughter was a revelation and it had been so long.

"You stepped in, when that kid had no one," he said, feeling a sudden swell of warmth for this woman. For her brave face and all her heart.

I love you, he thought. *More than ever.*

"Well, I don't think I did him any favors."

"How can you say that?"

"Because Nora Sullivan tore me a new one in my office ten minutes ago," she said, and then shook her head. "Let's…let's talk about something else. How was your morning?"

"Good. Louisa ate her weight in sausage, and Miguel had two shakes."

"I'll reimburse you."

"Stop, Juliette. I'm with you. I'm on your side. You don't owe me anything."

She looked at him a long time, her hazel eyes unguarded by glasses and for a second he felt naked—as if she could see through his clothes and skin to the heart that beat for her.

"Thank you," she said, sincere and warm, and he was touched by her genuine gratitude. "I should have said that before."

"You did."

"I didn't mean it."

Now he was laughing, and the good times between them were close enough to taste.

"Chief Tremblant," Nora Sullivan said, coming around the side of the porch with her hands on the shoulders of the two kids. The two smiling kids.

He heard Juliette gasp and they shared a startled look.

"I guess everything is okay?" Juliette asked.

Miguel just shrugged but Nora nodded. "We've set up some counseling sessions for the entire family. I am going to go find Mr. Pastor to set up a schedule and let him know what Miguel and Louisa have decided."

"What…what have you decided?" Juliette asked.

"We want to stay in our home," Miguel said. "But only if Dad stops drinking."

"And if he doesn't?" Juliette asked.

Miguel and Louisa shared a long look. "Ms. Sullivan says we won't be split up if we go into foster care, she knows someone who can take us together."

"Okay," Juliette said after a moment. She seemed slightly unglued and Tyler put his hand on her shoulder to steady her. The heat of her skin through her linen shirt melted him and he wanted to wrap himself around her warmth and not let go.

So, he forced himself to, taking his hand back and shoving it deep in his pocket.

He was happy for her, but this was her happiness.

"Ms. Sullivan," Juliette said, stepping away from Tyler. "I'll take you back to the station."

"And I'll put you two back to work," Tyler said.

Juliette and Nora Sullivan left, and as he led the kids away he couldn't help hugging Louisa to his side.

"I'm proud of you," he said to Miguel.

"I need to take care of my family," Miguel said, his eyes on his sister as she raced on ahead, looking for her tool belt.

"Ms. Sullivan," Juliette said, as they stood in the parking lot of the station, surrounded by cars and bird poop. "I can't thank you enough. You made a miracle happen—"

"No," Nora said, sliding her briefcase onto the hood of her car. She turned to face Juliette, unbuttoning her sleeves and rolling them up her arms in the midday sun. "He was scared of what he didn't know. I just told him the truth and let him make up his mind. I didn't let him dictate my actions."

"I'm sorry," Juliette said. "I was—"

"Scared. Like the kid. I understand. Trust me, I do." Oddly enough, Juliette had the sense that Nora did understand. "It is not my job to hurt kids or to break up families. I have to make every reasonable effort to prevent removal of children from their homes. It's my job to keep kids safe, and to that end, I appreciate what you've done. As wholly misguided and illegal as it was."

"You're not what I expected," Juliette said.

"I get that a lot. Look, call my office tomorrow and we'll set up some meetings." Nora tilted her head slightly, regarding Juliette carefully. "You and Miguel appear to be close."

Juliette nodded, leaning against her car, not feeling as if she was under scrutiny anymore. Feeling more as though she had found a powerful ally. "He and his sister are special kids. They just need someone to care." She let that sink in for a moment.

"You should consider being a foster parent," she suggested.

"Me?" Juliette asked, the idea shocking the hell out of her, so much so that she said the most asinine thing that sprang into her head. "I'm not married—"

"You don't need to be," Nora said. "You need to meet the qualifications and fill out the application. I would be willing to write you a letter of recommendation."

Juliette gaped. "You would? But the letter in my file—"

"Will still be there, with some qualifications." She lifted a finger. "We're a small parish and I've got seventeen kids in eight foster homes. We're strapped. And a woman like you is the kind of person we need. Someone who cares enough to put the kids first. With some training and some help, you'll be perfect. And considering that Miguel and Louisa have a fairly high likelihood of being put into foster care, it would be good to have a place with someone they know and trust."

"But you said you knew of someone who would take them both."

Nora's smile was sly and realization dawned.

"That's sneaky. What if I didn't want to be a foster parent?"

"I have a hunch about you, Chief Tremblant," she said,

and opened up her briefcase while Juliette turned over the idea in her head.

It was nothing she had ever considered. Ever. But she would know that Miguel and Louisa were safe, that they had a future they deserved and that she would be a part of it.

Thinking of watching them grow up, being privy to their lives, their adulthood, thrilled her, filled her with a big fat warm glow.

And then of course, maybe, in time—twenty or so years—she could win back Miguel's trust.

"Think about it," Nora said, handing Juliette a blue folder with the words *So You're Thinking About Being a Foster Parent?* printed on the front.

I am? she thought. And the idea took hold, gripping her with such force she wanted to shout.

Yes. I am.

LATER THAT WEEK, JASPER Tremblant was staring down at the low-fat, low-sodium, low-taste gumbo Juliette had made for their Sunday night dinner.

"This isn't étoufé," he said.

"Étoufé is all butter, Dad."

"When it's done right, yeah." Dad looked affronted and Juliette tried hard not to sigh. She spread her napkin over her lap and scooted in closer to the dining room table.

Aside from these weekly dinners, the napkins were usually balled up in a drawer and the table was lost under books and bills. But Dad liked a little pomp and circumstance. Or maybe he expected it. Or maybe she thought he liked it and so she did it.

She didn't know anymore.

All she was truly aware of was the slight dread she felt

about these nights. The apprehension that had long ago replaced any of the excitement she might have felt.

While she'd swept the floors, and cleared off her dining-room table, she'd wondered if this was how every woman of a certain age felt about her father.

Or if she and Dad were just special.

She'd wondered if things would be different if Mom were still around, but somehow she doubted it.

"Butter is off the menu, should have been a long time ago. I'm just trying to help you take better care of yourself." She dug into her dinner—if he didn't eat it, fine. Whatever. She couldn't make him do anything. He was an adult, even though he didn't always act like it.

"Thank you," he said, picking up his fork. "I'm sure it's delicious."

She gaped at him, watching him spoon a bite of gumbo into his mouth. Man, when he did things like that—criticizing one minute and apologizing the next—it threw her off. She could handle all of Dad's split personalities—Loving Dad, Suspicious Dad, Grouchy Dad—but every time he switched gears unexpectedly between his many incarnations, she was left flat-footed.

"You all right?" he asked. "You seem…distracted."

Distracted. Sleepless. Confused. Sometimes hopeful. Usually worried. She was a delightful mix of all the worst emotions and she wanted to climb right out of her skin.

In the past week, she'd attended the first two foster parent orientation meetings and she'd sent off her paper-work with letters of recommendation from Nora, Gaetan and teachers from the Academy. Now she had to wait for the home visit.

But that wasn't all.

Tyler O'Neill was back in her life, back in her head,

and she didn't know what to do about it, how to get rid of him.

Her father was right. She wasn't to be trusted around that man, because every day she went and picked up Miguel, and every day she had to tell herself that Tyler hadn't changed. Not really. Despite appearances. Tyler was a master of reflection—of showing people what they wanted to see.

And apparently she wanted to see a changed Tyler, which was just nuts. Crazy. Suicidal.

Tyler O'Neill turned her into someone else, someone she didn't know and didn't like.

I need an exorcism.

"I'm fine, Dad," she said with a smile, wishing she could tell her father everything and he could make it all go away. "Just tired."

"You doing some light reading?" Dad asked, pointing to the two giant juvenile psychology textbooks she had stacked at the end of the table.

"Yeah." She shrugged. "I've made myself family officer."

"Family what?" Jasper asked, setting down his spoon, sitting back with a serious air of disapproval.

She explained, as calmly as she could, the new aspect of her job, all while he sat across from her like a growing storm cloud.

"Is this about that boy you've got working out at The Manor? The boy who tried to steal that car?"

"Now." She sat back, her nerves on edge. "How do you know that?"

"The whole town knows, Juliette," he said, spearing a shrimp, his fork grating against the bottom of the bowl.

"Yes," she said through her teeth, bracing for the lecture. "It is about Miguel. It's about Miguel and the rising juvenile crime rate in Bonne Terre."

He nodded but didn't say anything. His thin nose practically twitched with his displeasure, but she took it as a small victory that he managed to keep his mouth shut.

But it couldn't last. Didn't.

Within moments, he threw down his fork and glared at her.

"I thought that boy was going to be taken to DOC!"

"Why in the world would—" She stopped, a terrible, terrible idea forming in her head. "No," she breathed.

"You can't protect the criminals, Juliette."

"It was *you*," she gasped, the fork clattering out of her hand. She couldn't catch her breath. Anger and hurt obliterated any brain function. "*You* called the Office of Community Services."

"You couldn't keep what you were doing a secret forever," Jasper said. "I was trying to help."

"Help!" she cried. Her father was insane, there was no other explanation. Somewhere along the way his love for her had gotten completely destroyed by his job.

"I could have lost my job!" she cried, and he brushed away her concerns with an elegant wave of his hand.

"You wouldn't have lost your job," he said. "But you would have learned an important lesson about the nature of your job."

"Tell me," she asked, "who were you trying to hurt, Dad? Miguel, Tyler or me?"

"Listen to yourself, Juliette. Hurt you? By sending a troublemaking kid where he belongs? You're too attached. Too damn soft."

"That's not true, Dad. Not at all. I'm good at my job. Damn good. And the world has changed—"

"I know, I know police are supposed to counsel and hold hands—"

"We're supposed to help! We're supposed to be reasonable—"

"Reasonable? I suppose that would explain why Tyler O'Neill is still in town," Jasper said, leaning forward, his words a terrible slap.

Juliette breathed hard through her nose.

"Tyler O'Neill is in town because he's done nothing wrong."

"You know, in my day—"

"I know what you did in your day, Dad," she snapped. "You set Owens on him like some kind of thug."

"People like Tyler O'Neill need to be shown who's in charge, otherwise they run around taking things that don't belong to them. Same as that Miguel boy."

Juliette tilted her head, her skin cold and prickly with anger. "I'm sorry, are you referring to me as a thing?"

"You had no business sneaking around with him behind my back."

"And I wonder why I felt like I had to sneak," she said, sarcasm a sword she was swinging around recklessly. "You would never have found out if you hadn't come to The Manor that night," she said. "You let Owens hit him, Dad. Over something he didn't even do."

"You can be mad at me all you want," he said. "But that boy left you without a word. Without so much as a goodbye."

The pain and embarrassment was a fast-moving storm, taking her by surprise.

"Regardless, Dad, you're wrong about Tyler—"

"Wrong? Listen to yourself. You think he's changed? You think a man like that can change?"

The words stuck pinpricks into her secret heart, where

she carried that damning belief, that terrible wish that he was changing. She had to battle the impulse to tell her father about the land outside of town, the houses he was going to build, the way he'd helped her with Miguel and Louisa. The way he made her laugh again, when she thought the whole world was dark.

But her father would only use it as further proof that she had no perspective when it came to Tyler O'Neill.

And maybe she didn't.

"He should be given the chance to," she said, and stood up, her anger a bright star on a dark night, leading her in the right direction. "And you stepped way over the line when you called OCS about Miguel. I think you need to leave."

"Leave?" He smiled. "Come on, honey. We're just—"

"Leave!" she cried.

The silence was stunning, painful, a gauntlet she had to get through, but finally he stood, putting his napkin on the table.

"I have only wanted the best for you," he said. "And I know you thought it was a secret, but I knew something was happening with you that summer. You were beginning to talk about not attending Oklahoma, about changing your plans for law school. I knew that wasn't my daughter talking."

"Go," she said, and then watched her father's back as he left her home.

Her father was wrong about so many things, but there was one thing she could not deny.

Falling in love with Tyler was like having her life realigned. And, stupidly, she could feel it all happening all over again.

And that had to stop.

Her father was right. She was making up what she

wanted to see, creating a Tyler O'Neill myth, just like she used to, because a man so beautiful, a man who could make you feel so good, couldn't be bad. Couldn't be rotten.

But he was. For her, he was all wrong.

And it was time to for him to leave.

CHAPTER TWELVE

MONDAY MORNING, JULIETTE GOT a message from Tyler that he was going to take Miguel out to watch the bulldozers clear out the FEMA trailers.

A few hours later, unable to keep her mind on work, she took the drive out to the site. Only to find Tyler alone next to his truck.

"Where's Miguel?" Juliette asked, yelling over the sounds of bulldozers and jackhammers breaking up the concrete pads.

Tyler pointed to the bulldozer systematically rolling over a brown trailer that used to be someone's home. From inside the cab, wearing a hard hat and sitting next to a man she recognized as Bill Hartley, Miguel waved.

The smile on the kid's face could light up the night sky.

Tyler did this, she thought, amazed. He brought on that smile and he's actually going to build houses out here.

"Cool, huh?" Tyler yelled, his eyes twinkling in a way that made her knees tremble, her heart pound.

Anger was what she wanted. Anger was safe. Anger was where she belonged.

But she just couldn't seem to hold on to it.

"Can we talk?" she yelled, unwilling to have this conversation at decibels that hurt.

He nodded and spun on his heel, opening the door of his truck. "Inside," he mouthed, and she followed suit.

They slammed the truck doors shut and the roar outside was diminished. But now, the air was suddenly too warm. Tyler sat too close. The memory of that kiss a week ago and the thousands that preceded it were now front and center.

Why are we doing this in a car? she wondered. It reminded her far too much of all the time they'd passed in the back of another car ten years ago.

You are here, she reminded herself, *for answers. Not to lust.*

"You want a cookie?" Tyler asked, picking up an open box from between them on the floorboards. "I got weaseled into buying twenty-five boxes of Girl Scout cookies from Louisa."

"I've got ten at home," she said, trying not to smile.

"That girl." Tyler shook his head and dug four cookies out of the box before handing them over to her. "Keep her away from politics."

She took two that she didn't want, but was happy to have something to do with her hands besides reach out and brush away the white thread hanging on to his tanned forearm.

"We need to talk," she said.

"We do," Tyler said, licking at the cream center of one of the cookies as if he was in a porno or something. "I want to offer Miguel an afterschool job out here. You know, around his counseling sessions."

She was taken aback, all filthy thoughts fleeing the cab of his truck. "You do?"

"Yeah." Tyler laughed. "The kid is talented. He's practically building that porch at The Manor by himself and his geometry skills—" Tyler whistled. "I think Derek and the other trades could really teach him something. You know? Something useful. Of course he—"

Nora Sullivan's words about Tyler O'Neill being the

seed of her community service program whispered in her head.

"When are you leaving?" she practically barked, not nearly as calm as she wanted to be.

He blinked, blinked again, and suddenly all his excitement vanished into cold understanding.

"You going to run me out of town?" he asked. "Like father, like daughter?"

"I'm just thinking you're probably getting itchy feet."

Tyler stared out the window and Juliette could see the pounding of his heart under the skin of his throat.

"What if I told you I wasn't leaving?" he murmured. Juliette went totally and utterly still. She'd come here seeking answers, but had hoped not to hear this one.

Now what are you going to do? she asked her shell-shocked self.

"I'm sticking around," he said. "I want to see Katie and Savannah. I want to meet this guy she loves. I…I'm staying in Bonne Terre."

"What exactly do you plan on doing here?" she asked, the words painful in a too-tight throat.

"I'm rich," he said with a careless shrug. "I don't need to do anything."

"You're just going to lie around all day? Play piano out at Remy's all night?"

Tyler stretched his arm across the top of the seat, his fingers inches from her hair. She tried not to notice the distance between their bodies, but her skin was doing its own calculations. Every millimeter between them was mapped out and noted so that she couldn't breathe without knowing how it brought them closer.

She shifted away and he noticed, his sharp eyes not letting her get away with anything.

"Actually, I thought Miguel and I could start a car theft ring. He could steal them, I'd chop them up for parts."

"You're hilarious," Juliette said. "Be serious."

"Christ, Juliette, it's no big deal. I thought I'd play piano at night," he said. "Get to know my niece and my sister. Help Margot around the house. I've given this community a lot of money over the years, and Remy and Priscilla are getting old. It's hard enough running Remy's at their age. I think if I want to keep helping people here, I'm going to need to do some of this stuff myself."

She refused to be moved. Refused.

Sunlight sparkled around them, catching dust motes and turning the air into glitter. Such was the power of Tyler O'Neill, and she suddenly realized much to her sick astonishment he was showing her the real him. No bluff. No sleight of hand.

He wasn't a mirror reflecting what she wanted.

It was him.

Just him. The real Tyler O'Neill.

And he destroyed her.

"You lied to me," she said.

Tyler squinted up into the sunshine and nodded. "Several times, but what are you referring to, specifically?"

"You're not an asshole at heart."

He was quiet while the crunch and smash of machinery rolling over metal echoed all around them.

"I think," he said, looking at her, his face utterly composed, his eyes rock solid, "I'm trying to change my ways."

There was nothing she could say to that. Because, despite the proof he'd offered her to sway her toward belief on one side of the scale, all she had was the cynical proof he couldn't change—proof that took the shape of heartbreak.

"You don't believe me?" he asked.

"Do you blame me?" she asked, her throat and mouth a desert.

"No, I don't. You have every reason to hate me," he said. "But hating me doesn't explain why you're here. Why you care."

She ignored his implications. "Where's your girlfriend?" she finally managed to ask. "The French model in all the magazines?"

"Theresa Guerriere," he said. "She dumped me."

She didn't even bother to try and keep her mouth closed. He smiled at her expression. "I'm not kidding," he insisted, and then suddenly the sparkle drained away and Tyler suddenly looked older. Tired. She was able to see Margot in him, and even Savannah. And not just the eyes and the hair, but the careful side of the O'Neills. The wary side that curled up around their hurts so other people couldn't see.

It was human. Real. Devastating.

"She thought she was pregnant," he said, and the air emptied out of Juliette, and she was just a sack of skin and incredulity. "And I...I was so damn happy. So..." He blew out a big breath. "Ready to be a person. A real person. A human with family and a home. I proposed."

"Marriage?" she squeaked. The concept of marriage and Tyler sharing space in the same sentence practically made her head explode. Jealousy gnawed at her bones.

"I proposed—" he glanced at her sideways, his grin a stab at her heart "—marriage. And she said no because she got her period. And she had no intention of being a person with a family and a home. Not with me."

So much pain. It just radiated off of him, soaking into her skin by osmosis. "Did you love her?" she whispered.

He winced. "No," he said slowly. "I loved the idea of a

baby. But Theresa and I were really more of an arrangement than a couple. In the end, we were lucky she wasn't pregnant. It would have been a disaster between us."

She didn't know what to say, how to process this new man beside her. She twisted a cookie in her hands, tearing it apart and then putting it back together.

"What about you?" he asked.

"What about me?"

"Any proposals?" he teased. The glitter was back, but not completely. She'd seen behind the curtain and the mighty and powerful Oz was just a man with hurts and pains, like the rest of the world.

It was a sickness on her part that it made him even more attractive to her.

"No," she said. "No proposals."

"You happy being chief?"

"Sure," she said.

"What happened to law school?"

"I got impatient," she said. She pressed her finger down on a black cookie crumb on her pants and touched it to the tip of her tongue. "I wanted to get on with my life, get to work, and law school was going to take forever. I got my masters at night while working."

He chuckled and looked at his hands. "Patience was never your strong suit."

"No." She smiled. "It still isn't. But it's something I'm working on."

"Have you always worked in Bonne Terre?"

"No, I've only been here six months," she said. "I was a lieutenant in Baton Rouge for a long time. I had gotten my masters in Municipal Administration and was thinking about a change when Dad retired and the interim chief they'd hired didn't work out."

"So you decided to come home and fill your father's

shoes?" There was a world of sarcasm behind his words, but instead of getting angry, she understood where it came from.

She looked at him, the softness and magic of him, and remembered that night when Owens came after him and how ugly it had gotten. How violent.

She'd told herself she'd never apologize to him for her father's mistakes, but maybe some of Dad's mistakes were hers, too.

"I'm sorry," she whispered. "That night—"

He put his hand on hers, setting her ablaze from her fingers, across her hand to her arm. Her heart exploded into flames and she had to pull away.

"I know," he said, quick and earnest. "I remember that night. I remember what you sacrificed for me."

"Sacrificed?" she choked, remembering the blood on Tyler's lip, the hate in her father's eyes. "Telling my father that you were with me and not stealing computers out of the high school wasn't a sacrifice—I should have told him about us months before."

"It would have saved me a bloody nose," he said, his smile holding no rancor, no grudge. Owens, on her father's okay, had made a mess of Tyler's face that night, and he didn't blame her for keeping him a secret. He never had.

Funny that she never realized how noble that was until right now.

She looked at him, everything suddenly so clear, the years of hurt and anger not blurring the focus. And the conversations she had with her father suddenly made sick sense.

"What did my father do?" she gasped.

Tyler quickly shook his head, and that he understood exactly what she was talking about damned her father with guilt. "Nothing, Juliette. I was a kid and I was scared." His eyes were dead serious. "Leaving you was my mistake."

His words shook her. "Mistake?" she asked on a weak breath of air.

He stared at his hands for a long time and she held her breath, waiting. When he finally looked up at her, his eyes were as blue and bright as if they were made out of the hottest part of flame.

"I told you the truth the other night at Remy's," he said. "I have thought about you almost every day for the past ten years."

She licked her dry lips with a drier tongue, trying desperately to process all of this in a way that wouldn't implode her life. But it didn't seem possible. Nothing was ever going to be the same again, not after this conversation.

"But why did you leave that way?" she finally asked. "Without a word?" She could forgive so much, but that seemed too heartless.

Tyler flexed his fingers and made fists. She ached to touch those hands, to feel them against her skin again, the bite of them in her flesh.

"Because I knew you would have left with me," he said, and the truth of his words blew a thousand holes right through her. "You would have thrown away law school and your future to be with me. And—" He shook his head. "That would have been your mistake."

"So you made the decision for me?" she asked, anger overtaking sadness and disbelief. "How dare you? It's *my* life—you don't get to make those kinds of decisions for me."

"We were kids, and you had a future. I had a beat-up Chevy and some luck at cards."

"Your piano," she whispered. "The music. You were going—"

"To support us by playing the piano?" he scoffed, and it felt like sandpaper over her heart. "It was better that I left. You may not see it, but that's the only option we had then."

"I don't see it that way, Tyler. I would have stood up to my dad."

He was silent for a long time before responding. "You know it's easy to say that, even to think it. But actually doing it?" He looked at her. "Putting aside your blood... it's hard. It changes you, Juliette."

"You did it," she said. "Margot, Savannah. You walked away from them."

"Which is why I can't do it again," he muttered. "My dad..." He shook his head and she understood why he kept the man around, despite the pain he'd caused. He was the only family Tyler had left—without Richard, he had no one.

"That's why you're staying," she said. "Your dad?"

"Someone has to look after him." He looked up at her, right through her. "But he's only part of the reason."

The question she didn't want to ask ripped its way from her heart, leaving behind a thousand cuts that would never heal.

"Are you staying for me?" she asked.

Tyler looked up at the sun, over to Miguel in the distance, and all the while Juliette held her breath, knowing the answer and not wanting to hear it.

Don't say it, Tyler. Don't make this happen. Don't put us here.

"Would you have me?" he whispered.

She gasped, as if taking her last breath before drowning in cold, cold water.

She fumbled with the door, needing to be out of there

before her heart spoke for her. "I need to go," she said. "I need to get Miguel and pick up Louisa."

His hand on the bare skin of her arm froze her. Her entire body felt the press of those fingers, the heat of that palm. She closed her eyes, swamped, utterly overrun by sensation.

"You're running," he said. His thumb grazed the sensitive skin of her elbow. Her body loosened its boundaries, relinquished its control. It's what he always did to her. It's what she'd always wanted him to do to her and she wanted it again. Now.

"Answer me, Jules."

She couldn't, afraid of what would spill out if she opened her lips.

"I know you feel something," he murmured. His fingertips brushed her cheek, the corner of her lip, and she wanted to hoard the sensation, the electric pulses and shocks. "I know I'm not alone."

You're not, she thought. *You never were.*

"I don't know," she said, looking up at him with old eyes. She was no longer Chief Tremblant. She was Jules, a girl in love.

"Juliette?"

"I'll think about it."

JULIETTE CHARGED PAST the white columns out front of her parents' home. She knocked once on the big black door with the lion's head knocker and then just went on in, powered by an engine of anger.

"Dad!" she yelled.

There was a thump upstairs and she walked across the checkered foyer to the bottom of the curving mahogany staircase. This house had been in Momma's family for generations, and without her in it, the place seemed like a museum. Dad just didn't have the power to fill it like Momma used to.

"What's happening, Juliette?" Dad asked, coming to stand on the landing, his elegant face creased with worry.

The anger in her doubled at the sight of him.

"What did you do to Tyler ten years ago to make him leave?"

Dad frowned, as if the question didn't make sense. "I don't know what you mean."

"Cut the crap!" she cried, gripping the balustrade so hard her fingers ached. "I know you did something that night, or Owens did something worse than a bloody nose. What was it?"

Dad stepped down the rest of the stairs, back straight, eyes focused as though he was taking her out on her first cotillion again.

"Ten years ago is a long time," he said. "It's possible no one really remembers the truth."

She narrowed her eyes. "You don't forget anything, Dad," she said. "What did you do?"

"I gave him a nudge," he said, with one of his long-suffering sighs. "That's all. A point in the right—"

"Stop the riddles," she sighed. "Look, I know since Mom died you and I—" Dad tensed, but she pressed on. "You and I haven't always seen eye to eye. And maybe me coming back to be chief wasn't the best idea, but I'm an adult, Dad. And you need to tell me the truth."

He didn't say anything, he didn't even move. Or twitch.

"If you don't say something, I am going to walk out that door and I swear I won't—"

"I gave him his father's address in Las Vegas. I told him to find his way and to let you find yours."

Juliette rocked back on her heels, all too able to imagine what Tyler would have felt, faced with that information. Tyler, whose whole life had been steered by missing parents.

"Is that all?"

Dad shrugged. "I might have indicated that life would get more difficult for him if he stayed."

"Difficult?" she asked. "What exactly is that code for, Dad? You'd continue to sic Owens on him? You'd arrest him? His grandmother? Maybe his little sister?"

"Maybe!" he cried, his righteous poise cracking. "They're the O'Neills, Juliette. Every single one of them is trouble. But leaving was Tyler's choice, Juliette. He left on his own—"

She bit her tongue and swallowed her anger. "He was a kid, Dad. And you were abusing your power."

His eyes got wide. "I was doing what a police chief and a father does. I was protecting the good citizens from the bad."

Juliette was suddenly so weary of this battleground. They never got anywhere and the land between them was scorched and ruined. If they kept at this, there would be nothing left. Nothing worth salvaging.

More and more she looked at him and he was a stranger.

"You need to stay out of my life, Dad," she said. "And out of my job. Can you do that?"

"I'm not in your—"

"You don't even see what you do, do you?" she asked, so sad, full of disbelief that their relationship was coming to this impasse.

They stared at each other a long time.

"I don't know how to answer that," he whispered.

"I know you don't, Dad," she said, and turned away.

"I'm sorry," he said, stepping after her. Reluctantly, she turned. "I'm sorry for calling OCS. You're right, it wasn't my place."

She rocked back slightly, stunned by the apology.

"And I know…I can be tough, but you're all I have left," he said, so small in his big empty house. "I don't want to lose you, too."

"You might be too late," she said, as honest and blunt as she could be, because she had nothing else to give him. "You might be ten years too late."

She left, her boot heels like gunshots in the empty foyer.

In the car she couldn't find her keys. Once she found them, she couldn't get them into the ignition. Her hands didn't work, her whole body shook.

She dropped her keys, put her head on the steering wheel.

Just like that, she understood. She understood why he'd thought what he had ten years ago. Why he'd left and even why he hadn't told her. Because he was right—she would have gone with him. In a heartbeat.

And even though he was wrong, he thought he was doing the best thing for her. He thought he was protecting his family, and even more, he thought he might finally find his father. A piece of his puzzle he'd been missing his whole life.

He'd been eighteen, manipulated by a man who should have known better. Who should have been above hurting a kid like that.

In the end, it was easy. Ten years of anger. Of hurt. It all rode out on a long breath.

"Tyler," she sighed.

I forgive you.

CHAPTER THIRTEEN

LATER THAT NIGHT, JULIETTE sat on her couch—her stomach in knots, her head turning circles—and waited as long as she could. She ate the last bit of ice cream in her freezer, contemplated getting more, but then settled for chocolate chips. By the handful.

She organized her socks with one eye on the clock.

Eleven-forty-five.

Balanced her checkbook.

Midnight.

The darkness in her living room grew purple at the corners, street traffic died down and it felt as though it was just her and the quiet world and every thought of Tyler she was trying to avoid.

He's staying? Really?

For me?

And I'm considering it?

She was losing her mind.

Finally, at one-fifteen in the morning, she picked up her phone.

It was 8:15 a.m. in Paris, a disgusting time to call a friend on the most romantic vacation of her life, but Juliette was desperate. More than desperate—she was frantic.

And Savannah, she knew, was an early riser. And forgiving.

"Come on, come on," she muttered as the signal connected and buzzed its way across the ocean to Savannah's cell.

"Hello?"

"Savannah," Juliette sighed, so happy and relieved to hear her friend's voice she nearly cried. "Did I wake you?"

"No, but—" There was a rustle and a murmur. The sound of a kiss and Juliette winced, imagining the sweet scene she was interrupting. "What are you doing calling so early?" Savannah's voice echoed and Juliette guessed her friend just snuck off into the bathroom. "It's the middle of the night there."

"I need to talk to you."

"Apparently. What's up? Everything okay at The Manor?"

"Tyler's there."

"Where?"

"At The Manor."

"Really?" Savannah asked, sounding like the ten-year-old girl she always turned into when talking about her brothers. "He came home."

"Worse, Savvy. He's staying."

"Until we get back?"

"Longer."

"That's fantastic!" Savannah cried. Juliette heard a door open. "Guess what, Katie. Uncle Tyler's home!" There was a squeal, the rumble of Matt's laugh, and then Juliette heard the door close again. Savannah clearly did not understand the reality of this situation. "Wait a second," Savannah said. "He's not looking for the gems, too, is he?"

"No," Juliette answered, distracted by the question. Good God, she'd practically forgotten about those gems. That was the effect Tyler had on her. "You're missing the point. He won't stay," Juliette said, her words harsh, a reminder to herself more than a warning to her friend.

"I mean, I hate to burst your bubble, but you know your brother won't stick around."

"I don't know, Juliette. He's a grown man now, not a kid. If he says he's staying, I think he'll stay."

"Of course you do!" Juliette snapped. "You always want to believe the best about Tyler despite all evidence that he's a lying bastard."

There was a long pause and Juliette closed her eyes. "Sorry. I keep forgetting the lying bastard is your brother."

Savannah laughed, which was one of the many reasons why Juliette loved her. "Has something happened between you two?"

Other than the fact that he seduced me, told me he loved me and deserted me ten years ago?

She stared up at her ceiling, the white stucco giving her no answers. No solace. Everywhere she looked, there he was. Everywhere she turned there was possibility. "He says he's staying…for me."

"Oh. Wow."

"Yeah. Wow."

"What did you say?" Savannah asked.

Juliette closed her eyes and related the impossible. "That I'd think about it."

"Wow, I picked a crazy time to go on vacation."

"He hurt me so bad, Savannah. I can't…I can't do that again."

"You know, Jules, ten years is a long time. Maybe Tyler's different."

Juliette snorted, thinking about Tyler lying about his father being at The Manor. She couldn't forget that. Or ignore it. He'd lied to her—repeatedly.

"And *you're* different," Savannah said. "You're not that trusting love-struck girl anymore."

"And whose fault is that?"

"I'm just saying, if you're different and you still feel this way, maybe he's different and feels the same way, too."

Juliette had nothing to say to that, torn between hope and a probable reality.

"If it makes you feel better, I think he stayed away all these years because of you," Savannah said.

"How in the world is that supposed to make me feel better?"

"Well, I don't think he abandoned you because he didn't love you."

"I know," she whispered, thinking of her father's confession.

The truth was, Tyler had been a kid, bullied by a police chief and tempted by something he'd always longed for—a father. A family.

If she'd been in his shoes, she couldn't say she'd have resisted. And that understanding changed everything.

"You know, Juliette, one thing I'd never call you is a coward," Savannah said.

"Or a fool," Juliette said.

"Well, that, too. But that's the trade-off—love isn't safe."

Don't I know it.

But she wasn't a coward, and if Tyler could risk himself like he had, over and over again, throwing himself against the sharpest edges of her anger—couldn't she man up and meet him halfway?

She'd loved Tyler like she'd never loved another man—and never would, that much was clear. Didn't the possibility of keeping that love warrant a little risk?

A little courage?

There would have to be an understanding, she thought, galvanized by purpose. About him keeping things from her.

And they would go slow. Carefully.

"Juliette? I have to get going," Savannah said. "Are you okay?"

No, she thought, *but I will be.*

Maybe.

THAT NIGHT, TYLER SAT cross-legged on the floor of the attic, a box of Savannah's book reports open in front of him like a treasure chest. He was lost on page three of a grade-school science report on penguins. Apparently, her favorite animal.

He didn't know that.

He didn't know that if she could go back in time she'd go to Paris in the 1800s. Or that her favorite book in third grade was *Little House on the Prairie.*

All this paper, yellowed and soft with age, the pen fading to pencil as he went deeper into the box, carried clues about a sister he didn't really know.

But he was determined to find out. To stick around and know her.

His future was wide-open and dusted with possibilities. He had a chance to make amends and earn back the family he'd left behind.

"You find anything?" Richard asked, his head poking up through the crawl space.

"No gems," Tyler answered without looking up. Even as a kid, Savannah's research was so freaking thorough, no wonder she became a professional researcher; it was like a gift or something.

"I'm thinking I must have missed something in the—"

"They're not here, Dad," he said, turning a page in the report only to find a drawn diagram of a penguin, adorable in its crudity. "We've been through every inch of this house. Every inch. And there are no gems."

Richard wiped his forehead, leaving a trail of cobwebs and dust. "You might be right. But we haven't really searched the—"

"I am right," Tyler said, setting the report neatly back into the box. "This search is done. It should have been done before it even started, but as of now—" He put the lid back on the box and shoved it into its space in the eaves. He pulled out another box simply marked Katie.

A niece that he barely knew.

"It's over," he finished.

He tore off the lid. Dust and baby powder wafted up to him, a smell so foreign it could have been frankincense and myrrh.

"What you got there?" Richard asked, pulling himself up into the attic. The boards creaked and Richard paused, as if waiting for the floor to give up under him.

"Baby things," Tyler said, taking out a pink blanket and what looked like a well-loved stuffed rabbit missing an ear. It was sticky, but smelled good, like jelly and baby shampoo. "Katie's."

It had been a few years since he'd seen his niece, but saying her name brought back the sensation of her hand in his, that wild-child spark in her eyes. He'd taken her down to the restaurant in the hotel where he'd been living and they'd had pancakes for dinner, ice cream for breakfast. He'd taken her swimming in the big wave pool and taught her to float on her back, her little belly sticking up like an island out of the water.

Tyler put the rabbit by his knee, pulling out a tiny pink baby hat and a hospital band.

Hope was a rocket he forced himself to sit on. Juliette hadn't turned him down today, hadn't laughed or smacked him. Instead, she'd stared at him with dry and level hazel eyes, and said she didn't know.

It wasn't a yes, but it sure as hell wasn't a no, and that was all that mattered.

Though he wished, he really wished, that Katie was here. That Savannah was here. Margot. All of the women in his life that he'd neglected and abandoned. They could join hands with Juliette and yell at him, or whatever they wanted to do, but they'd be here.

"That's my granddaughter," Richard said, pulling out from the box a picture of Katie and Savannah in the courtyard, back when it was a jungle.

Tyler snatched the photo out of his father's hands. "You've never even met her," he snapped.

"Blood is blood, Tyler."

"You sound like an idiot," Tyler said. "Laying claim to people you left behind, like you have the right."

"I was left," Richard said, indignant. "Your mother took you children away—"

Tyler was stunned by the lies Richard kept telling himself to make his pathetic life okay. Though Tyler had to admit, he used to do the same.

"Remember my first big win?" Tyler asked.

"Of course," Richard said, as if Tyler had won a college football game instead of taking people's money.

"You'd gotten me that fake ID and paid my way into that big game in Henderson. I won more money than I'd ever seen. You said, 'that's my boy,' and used my money to buy rounds for the bar."

Richard looked taken aback. "It's what you do—"

"It's what *you* do," Tyler said. "It's the Richard Bonavie way, and I ate it up."

But no more.

"You should think about moving on, Dad," he said,

stroking Katie's blanket, the fine weave catching on his newly calloused fingers. "The gems aren't here."

"Where should we go?" Richard asked. "Back to Vegas? Europe? I know a guy who runs a game outside of Paris."

Tyler looked up at him, Richard's face so familiar it might as well have been his own.

"I'm not going with you," he said. "I'm done."

Richard looked confused. "With what?"

"With that life. With gambling and stolen gems. I'm done with the Notorious O'Neills. I want something better."

"Done with it?" his dad asked, laughing. "Oh, so you're just going to be someone else now? Like it's that easy? You never graduated high school and you have no skills besides cards."

"I think you're getting us confused," Tyler bit out.

"Yeah, well, you and me, we ain't that different. You think you can just walk away from who you are, but trust me. Blood always wins out. I don't know shit about that Notorious crap—but you are who you are and you can't run from that."

Dad left the attic, slamming doors behind him.

Part of Tyler wanted to follow him, insist that his father was wrong. That his life was a choice, not a legacy. But there wouldn't be any point.

He was starting a brand-new life. Right now. This moment.

Tucking his niece's artifacts back in the box, Tyler's knuckles brushed something hard in the corner. He tilted the box to see.

At the bottom was a red velvet bag, shiny and worn with age and handling. An unraveling gold string kept the top pulled tight. A little girl's treasure bag, he thought fondly, wondering if he should pry into it.

Curiosity won out and he scooped it up, surprised at its heft. He loosened the string, tipped it into his palm, and the red bag burped out a giant thirty-karat diamond.

CHAPTER FOURTEEN

DUMB AND DEAF, TYLER STARED at the gem refracting rainbows across the dim attic.

Is this a joke? he wondered through the buzzing in his head.

The notorious part of your blood will always find you.

If this wasn't some kind of cosmic proof, he didn't know what was and it turned his stomach to lead. The hope that had been powering him since this afternoon sputtered and died.

He quickly ran over his options. He could hide the gem back in the box and pretend he'd never found it, but there was no guarantee that Dad wouldn't come hunting up here tomorrow.

Dad could *not* have this gem.

This can of worms could not be opened. Ever. Not if he wanted to keep Juliette.

How did this even get here? he wondered, not sure which of his family members put it here. His mother? She was the most likely. She might have hidden the gem here when she broke in last month, but the attic was nearly impossible to get to.

Margot? he wondered. But that didn't make any sense— she'd been paying Mom stay-away money for years. If she really wanted Vanessa to stay away, Margot could have just given her the diamond.

Either way, word could not break that this gem had been found in The Manor. His family would be torn apart.

Tyler tucked it into his pocket, the weight like a fiery coal in his pants. Downstairs, he paused, waiting for sounds from his father making dinner, but the house was quiet.

Good.

Tyler went into his room and tucked the gem into a pair of black socks and then into his duffel bag. It would be safe there until he figured out what to do.

FRIDAY, THREE WEEKS AFTER starting the porch project, it was finished. Tyler put his paintbrush back in the can just as Miguel tossed his roller into the tray.

They'd painted it white, bright new-tooth white, which actually only made the rest of the house look more shabby. Worn down.

"Wow," Miguel said, tilting his head. "I guess we should start on the house next, huh?"

"I didn't think a new porch would be such a big deal," Tyler answered. "But you've done a great job. You've got real talent as a carpenter."

Miguel shrugged as if it was no big deal, but Tyler could see the boy preening under the praise. "You know, those houses we're building are starting up pretty soon." Miguel's stillness was complete and Tyler got this wild sense of satisfaction, a total sureness that he was doing the right thing. "I could use you on a crew."

"A job?"

"Yup."

"A raise?"

"Probably not."

Miguel blinked and blinked again. "You don't have to be so nice to me."

Ah, kid, you're gonna break my heart. "I don't?" he joked.

"I tried to steal your car and I've been coming—"

"Stop, Miguel. It's been fun having you here. You're clearly a good kid and frankly, it's just a job," Tyler said. "A hard one. Do you want it?"

Miguel kicked at the edge of the porch, his hands wrapped up in the extra baggy edge of his shirt. "Yeah," he said. "Of course."

"Great! Now, I feel like we should celebrate."

"You want to play cards?" Miguel asked. "Whenever I feel like celebrating I play a little hold 'em."

"If nothing else, kid, you are persistent." He gave the kid's shoulder a shake. The boy had bulked up over the past three weeks. Between the food and the work, he'd become strong, was beginning to take the shape of a man.

"How about you come out to Remy's with me tonight? Have some crawfish, listen to music."

"I'm not old enough," Miguel said.

"Oh, trust me, it don't much matter out at Remy's. Not if you come with me."

The boy rubbed his cheek on the shoulder of his shirt. "I…I can't be away from Louisa that long," he said.

Tyler nodded. He'd forgotten about Louisa. "Of course. Then how about I go buy you a burger in town?"

"What about the chief?" Miguel asked. "She's gonna be here in a little while to pick me up."

"Oh, right," Tyler said. "Well, she can come, too."

"You guys still fighting?" Miguel asked.

"We were never fighting," he lied.

"You know what girls like?"

"This should be good."

"They like it when you tell them they have a nice butt. They pretend they're offended, but they secretly love it."

"You think I should tell the Chief of Police she has a nice butt?" Tyler asked.

"Worth a shot."

Tyler howled. "Call her. Tell her to meet us."

IN THE PARKING LOT OUTSIDE of Ed's, Juliette put on lipstick, ran a brush through her hair. Smelled her armpits.

And she took it all as proof that she was losing her mind.

Primping for Tyler O'Neill.

Again.

She was about to sit across those cracked red Formica booths and try not to touch her leg to his. Try not to brush her fingers with his, and she was going to die a little every minute.

Nothing, absolutely nothing good could come of this.

At some point over the past few days, a slew of confusing and conflicted emotions and feelings had walked in the door forgiveness had opened.

Desire, for one. A big one.

Curiosity, another. Curiosity to see if it would be the same between them, as hot and consuming and mindless as she remembered.

And once she'd started thinking about hot and consuming and mindless sex with Tyler O'Neill, she'd been unable to stop. Which left her here, primping like a teenager.

She stepped out of her car, slamming the door behind her, and looked right into the laughing gaze of Tyler O'Neill staring out the window from their old booth.

He'd seen her. Great. Just great.

She was nineteen all over again, catching Tyler's eye in this very place for the first time.

"You look beautiful," Tyler said when she walked in the door.

She didn't know how to take compliments anymore so she awkwardly nodded and blushed so hard her hair smoked.

The air smelled like fat and calories and her stomach practically leaped out of her body. It had been hours since her yogurt this morning. A kid in a paper hat and an ice-cream-splattered apron came and took her order for one of the Double Specials.

The kid seemed dumbstruck for a moment, such was the power of a little red lip gloss, and then shuffled off.

Without the boy there, her lips and tongue were heavy with all the things she needed to say.

I forgive you. I miss you. Can you make me feel like you used to?

"Where's Miguel?" she asked, and Tyler pointed behind her at the far booth.

Miguel sat, arm across the top of the seat, looking every inch like Tyler a decade ago—talking to two girls who couldn't seem to get a word out without giggling.

"Oh, boy," she muttered.

Tyler laughed. "We ordered and the second those girls walked in he was gone."

"You hurt?"

"Tremendously," he said, and pushed a red plastic cup filled with ice and soda at her. "Might as well drink this, Miguel won't notice."

She took the soda and felt as if she stood on the edge of a cliff, breathless and scared. There was so much to say and she didn't know how to start. Where to start.

She looked to Tyler for help.

The air between them sizzled. It was too hot to talk.

"So, we're done with the porch," he said, looking away, playing it cool.

She blinked, unable to change directions so quickly.

"That's…ah…that's great," she said.

Tyler nodded, stretching his own arm across the top of the bench seat. His was darker from all the hours spent outside, his hair bleached nearly white by the sun, and she had to force herself not to stare. Not to follow every curve of muscle and pulse of vein with her eyes.

"He's going to take the job I offered him."

"I expected he would."

"Has he told you how counseling is going?" Tyler asked, clearly unfazed by the pheromones in the air. "He won't tell me anything."

Talking business cooled her off and she managed to relax in her booth, stretching her legs out beside Tyler's. "I think it's helping Miguel and Louisa. Ramon is actually going to some of the sessions, too."

"Really?" Tyler asked, as surprised as Juliette had been when she'd heard.

"But he's still drinking. He spent the night in the drunk tank last weekend."

Tyler sighed heavily through his nose. "I wish we could get those kids out of there."

"I've applied to be a foster parent," she said, letting her little secret out into the light of day. Tyler's eyebrows hit his hairline.

"What?" she snapped. This is why she hadn't told anyone, because people would think she was crazy.

"That's a fantastic idea. I don't know why I didn't think of it. What's happening?"

"I have one more orientation meeting and then a home visit before I'm approved."

"Wow." Tyler smiled. "That seems fast. Is that fast?"

Juliette nodded. "Nora's helping me. She's worried about Miguel and Louisa, too."

"Nora Sullivan?" Tyler asked. "Are we talking about the same woman?"

"I know, but trust me, she's actually a big softie." Well, maybe *softie* was a bit of a stretch, but she certainly wasn't quite the bulldog she appeared to be.

"I'm proud of you, Juliette," he said, so serious, so earnest. "The world needs more police chiefs like you."

Without even thinking, she put her hand over his, like putting her palm on a fire. Small explosions blasted through her and she wanted more. Unwittingly, she wrapped her fingers around his palm, feeling the calluses and warmth. The life.

His eyes flickered shut for a moment, as if he felt it all, too, and he just couldn't bear it.

"I talked to my dad," she whispered, the words spilling out of her mouth like water from a fountain. "He told me what he did. Your father's address and everything. I understand why you left and I understand why you kept him a secret when you came back."

Tyler's throat bobbed and she could hear his breath sawing out of his lungs. The world had shrunk down to them. To the air between them. His eyes and her need to touch him.

"Will you tell me about finding him?" she asked.

He closed his eyes and pulled his hand away from hers, leaving her palm cold and empty. "You don't want to hear about it, trust me."

"You're wrong," she breathed, and grabbed his wrist, her fingers on his pulse. "I want to hear everything about the last ten years. Talk to me," she said, tilting her head, trying to smile. "I used to have to beg you to shut up, remember?"

His lip twitched.

"It was like you'd never talked to anyone before," she

said, laughing. "Some nights, I'd just put the phone on my pillow and take a little nap." A lie, they both knew it. She'd hung on his every word.

"I'd never talked to anyone like you," he said, his eyes roving over her face. "Never to anyone who listened like you."

"I'm listening now," she said. "Tell me how you found your dad."

After a long moment his thumb brushed her hand and his fingers curled around hers, holding her hand in his palm like a little bird. "He was in Vegas, just like your father said. He'd just won a big purse and he loved showing me what a big man he was. He let me move in and within six months the money was gone. He'd been kicked out of most of the games in town, so I started to play to support us, keep us off friends' couches." He shrugged. "We've been a happy little family ever since," he said, the sarcasm a cloud around him.

It hurt her, that sarcasm, because it didn't even begin to hide the pain.

"I'm sorry, Tyler," she said, and he held up his hand.

"Whatever happens, from now on, no more apologies," he said. "We were kids. Your father was wrong, I was wrong. And maybe, just a little bit, you were wrong—"

"Me?"

"Talking about giving up law school?" Tyler tsked his tongue.

"My decision," she said. "Not yours, not my father's. Mine."

"You're right. That was up to you," he said, waving his hands and absolving her of guilt. He wasn't joking. Again, the fact that he didn't hold a grudge just killed her.

Was there a chance? A real chance that this man was as good as she wanted to believe? Was the truth, the shining, diamond-hard truth buried under dirt and distraction, that he was a rare man? One who deserved her love and respect? Her adoration?

There was only one way to find out. She had to try.

"Then no more lies," she said. "I won't apologize anymore, but you can't keep anything from me anymore."

No lies? Tyler thought, his stomach bottoming out.

Like, I found a priceless stolen gem in my grandmother's attic? A gem that could implicate my whole family in who knows what kind of mess?

You can trust her, he thought, desperate because the weight of this gem was growing slightly intolerable. But one look at her face, so earnest, so firm and beloved, and he knew he could not get her wrapped up in this.

This gem was Notorious O'Neill business all the way.

"Is that so hard?" she asked. There was a smile on her lips, but he could see the balances in her eyes, the way things were tipping out of his favor the longer he waited.

He'd call Carter, should have done it yesterday. The two of them could figure this out. Make a plan. Ditch the diamond someplace where no one would ever find it.

She would never know.

"No lies," he said, and nodded. "I can do that."

Luckily the waiter showed up with a tray of food, preventing him from having to elaborate.

"Miguel!" Tyler called, waving him away from his girls.

The smell of cheese and bacon and pickles wafted up from the foil-wrapped treasures in front of them and Juliette dug in. Her appetite had always been one of those things Tyler loved about her. Watching her eat food had turned into one of the more erotic aspects of their relationship. He didn't even want to guess the number of ice cream cones he'd watched that girl demolish.

"Oh," Juliette groaned, and Tyler's body went hot. The woman even made a cheeseburger sexy. "Oh, that's good."

"Hey!" Miguel said, coming to stand at the edge of their table. "You drank my pop."

"You snooze, you lose," Juliette said, taking a big slurp.

"That's cold, Chief," Miguel said. "Cold."

Miguel reached over and snagged a handful of Juliette's fries and her smile was something new, or rather, something old. The old Juliette sat here, surrounded in sparkle and gold dust. His heart leaped and love flooded him.

Tyler felt removed for a moment, lifted away from the scene as if watching it from miles away. Juliette threw a French fry at Miguel, who reached over and stole another handful. She laughed and appealed to Tyler, but he could only smile.

A certain kind of fear trickled into Tyler's stomach. A fear that this was as close as he would get to real family— and that it could all be taken away from him.

A HALF HOUR LATER, MIGUEL LED them out of Ed's and high-tailed it right to the passenger seat of Juliette's car, his thumbs going to town on the keypad of his cell phone.

"He just said goodbye to them," Tyler said about the girls Miguel was no doubt texting. "Is he telling them about the parking lot?"

"It's Friday night," she said. "They're making plans he didn't want me to hear."

"Ah."

"Speaking of plans," she said, an awkward cheer in her voice, "are you at Remy's tonight?"

He nodded.

"Maybe…maybe I'll see you there," she said, her smile

flirty, as if they didn't have a million years of past between them. As if the threat of real heartache wasn't a lit fuse that could destroy them both. Again. He sobered.

"What are you doing, Juliette?" he asked.

"What do you mean?"

He reached out and turned her to face him, looking hard into her eyes, seeing every insecurity he felt. Every ounce of love and desire and fear.

"What are you doing, Juliette?" he whispered again and he knew, he could see it in her eyes, that she understood him.

"Do I have to know right now?"

He nodded. "I can't do casual, Juliette. Not with you."

She swallowed and he stepped closer, pushing his fingers into her hair. He could feel her heart hammer against the heel of his palm. The scent of lemons flooded him.

"If you come out to Remy's tonight," he murmured, "be prepared."

"For what?" she breathed.

"For me," he said, and pressed a whisper of a kiss against her sweet lips.

TYLER WALKED RAZOR WIRE all night. Believing she would walk in Remy's door at any moment and hoping, oddly, that she wouldn't.

Dying every time he looked up from the keys and saw that she wasn't there.

She's not coming.

How could she not?

You should be glad. Relieved.

I want her so much I can't stand it anymore.

Raquel, the singer, stopped singing and Mitch at the drum kit played his last fill when Tyler realized he was still playing the chords of the chorus.

"We're going to take a quick break," Raquel said, the perfect ebony of her skin absorbing the lights. The woman had shoulders like an archer and a voice like a songbird.

Maybe I should start something up with Raquel, he thought, sick of himself and Juliette and the past. *With Raquel I could do casual. And maybe casual is what I need. Maybe casual is all I'll ever need.*

"Ty," Raquel said, coming to stand between him and the crowd. "You with us tonight?"

"Right here," he muttered, lifting the hem of his shirt and wiping his forehead.

"The hell you are," Mitch said, his hand over the microphone.

"You're playing like the living dead," Raquel said, slightly more sympathetic. "If you need time—"

"I don't need time," he snapped. Everything in him was wound so tight he was about to burst. "I'm fine. Let's just keep playing."

She shook her head. "Baby, I don't let anyone make me look bad, and you are walking real close to that line."

He sighed. Freaking prima donnas. "Hey, you take care of you and I'll—"

Behind Raquel he caught a glimpse of jet-black hair, skin like cocoa. He leaned back, his heart a jackhammer against his ribs.

In the middle of the emptying dance floor, in a red dress that told him every secret her body ever wanted kept, was Juliette.

He stood, the bench screeching against the stage.

"Ty!" Raquel cried as he leaped off the stage.

Everything vanished, Raquel, Mitch, the rest of the set—the entire world just disappeared and it was Juliette. Right here.

Right now.

CHAPTER FIFTEEN

DESIRE LIKE SHE HADN'T felt in ten years hit her like a freight train. He leaped off the stage and crossed the empty dance floor, stalking her like some kind of jungle animal. His khaki pants hung low, his white tank top was damp and stretched at the bottom, like he'd been wiping his face with it all night. Beneath his beat-up fedora, his eyes burned holes through her dress until she stood there naked for him.

Mindless to anything but him.

Ten years of missing him and wanting him and trying to cool the fire that raged in her with lesser men exploded inside of her.

Here. Now. On the damn dance floor in front of everyone—it didn't matter. She needed Tyler's touch. She needed him, hard and high inside of her, touching places no one else ever seemed to find.

Finally, he was there, the smell of sweat and beer and sex rolling off of him. In his eyes there wasn't even a question. There was only happiness and delicious, delicious lust.

He grabbed her hand, his fingers twining with hers and the ache between her legs was so painful, so expectant, she wanted to scream.

There was nothing to say. No words that could make what was happening any clearer. She tugged on his hand, leading him toward the back patio where hardly anyone went.

The cool air was a gorgeous relief against her chest, bare legs and face for just one moment before the furnace of Tyler pressed against her back.

"You're here." His breath feathered across her neck and her nipples went so hard so fast, she gasped.

"You ready?" he asked, and she nodded, words beyond her.

"Tell me, Juliette," he said. "Say the words."

"I'm ready."

"For?"

Oh, man, she was going to fall apart. She was going to burn to ash. His fingertips brushed, just barely, against the skin of her breast.

"What are you ready for, Juliette?" he asked, his voice a purr, his fingers a feather against her ribs, her stomach.

She turned and looked him right in the eye. "You," she whispered.

He groaned and kissed her. She expected a devouring. Something wild and rough. But what she got was tender, reverent. Tyler O'Neill at his sweetest and most restrained, and it tore her apart like nothing else.

She pulled back to look into his face, taut with lust, with a rigid control that she loved and wanted to demolish at the same time. His hair, sun shot and rumpled, fell over his eyes.

He smiled, everything in him beaming out toward her, like arms reaching for her. Like love and laughter. Like a family. Like belonging.

And she fell. She fell right back into love with Tyler O'Neill.

"Look," he said. "Not that I'm about ten seconds from ripping that dress off you. But I understand if this is too fast—"

Honestly, how could I not love him? she wondered, awestruck by his grace.

"Is it too fast for you?" she asked.

His laugh was pained.

"I didn't think so." She reached for him, but his hands braced against her hips and held her away.

"No, Juliette," he whispered.

"No, what?" she asked, not comprehending, lust making a mess of her head.

"Not like this. We're not kids sneaking around anymore, are we?"

"No," she whispered. "We're not."

"Then let's do this right," he said. "Let's go back to your place."

"My place?" she asked. "Not your old single bed at The Manor?"

His eyelids flinched. "My dad's there," he said, and stroked her arm, raising gooseflesh up and down her body.

"I could meet him," she offered. She didn't particularly want to, but Priscilla's comments about pulling Tyler to good and bad pieces and only loving the good parts rang in her head. "You know…officially."

He shook his head. "I don't want him anywhere near you," he said. And she knew what he meant and wanted to protest—she wasn't something he needed to protect or keep clean. She was ready for him and all his skeletons.

His kiss burned away her noble thoughts and all she wanted was him alone for several hours. Getting to know the family could wait.

Stopping was torture, but she threw back her hair and took his hand.

"Let's go," she said.

TYLER FOLLOWED JULIETTE'S TAILLIGHTS to a little bunga-
low on a dark, tree-lined street. Curiosity over where and
how she lived fought a valiant battle against blood-boiling
lust, but as soon as he saw one long, elegant leg slide out
her car door, curiosity went down in flames.

He wanted her so bad he could barely breathe, much
less think. He was destroyed by her, turned to ash and
rubble.

He turned off his ignition and jumped out of the car,
getting to her just as she closed her own door.

She was gorgeous in the shadows, her hair an inky mystery. He touched a curl as it rested against her bare shoulder
and then slid his hands up until he cupped her head and
she gasped. Electricity surrounded them, crackling and
popping.

"Second thoughts?" he asked.

"No," she whispered. "Absolutely not."

"Good," he said, and kissed her. He nipped at her full
lips until they opened and his tongue touched hers.

She pushed against him. "I didn't drive all this way to
do this against my car," she muttered, her eyes flashing.

"Lead the way," he said, stepping back, but not letting
go of her hand.

They didn't bother with small talk, or light. She opened
her door, he kicked it shut. She led him through the dark
house and all he watched was the sway of her hips. She
could have been leading him to hell, for all he cared.

In the bedroom he got a quick impression of a purple
comforter and lingerie spilling out of an open dresser
drawer before she turned to face him.

She glowed in the shadows, lit from within by a fire
that he had longed to warm himself by for as long as he
could remember. He was humbled because she stood there

as a woman who frankly knew better than to get involved with him.

And she still chose him.

She grabbed the hem of his shirt, pulling it up over his head and throwing it on the floor. "Look at you," she breathed, her hands on his chest, the muscles of his stomach. "Tyler O'Neill, all grown up. You're like a statue."

He nearly laughed. Part of him sure felt like a statue.

He found the zipper under her arm and pulled it down, the dress rippling down to the floor. Suddenly, there she was. Juliette Tremblant in a whisper of black silk and shadows.

Her body was still so taut. Strong. Her breasts small but perfect, her hips a little bigger, rounder. Womanly. He ran a finger from her collarbone to the lace between her legs.

"I can't believe you let me touch you," he said, awed, curling his fingertip around the elastic and pulling it down just enough that dark curls appeared around his finger.

Juliette's breath hitched, her eyelids fluttered.

He knew this was fast, that there were a thousand steps he was missing, body parts he should get reacquainted with first, but her head tilted back and she gripped his wrist, urging him, ever so slightly, on.

He worked a finger through those curls to the hot little slit waiting for him. He felt her desire like humidity and he slid that finger just inside. To that hot spot.

She gasped, her knees buckling and she reached forward and grabbed his belt. He grazed her clitoris with the callus on his fingertip, the smallest touches and she reacted like he was using dynamite.

She leaned forward, resting her head against his chest, and he slid his finger deeper, finding the open well of her body. She moaned deep in her throat.

Something dark was building between them. Something hotter than anything they might have shared in the past.

He twisted his hand and another finger entered her and her hands cupped his shoulder, nails biting into his skin. With her other hand she tore at his belt, pawing at the fly of his pants until they puddled at his feet.

He kicked off his shoes, stepped free of his pants, and they were both naked, a shaft of moonlight slicing across them. His hand against the dark nest of curls was illuminated, her eyes, dilated and glowing with hunger.

Her hand slid down his arm to his waist and then curled around his shaft, her thumb circling the head of his penis, her fingers squeezing. He gasped against the pleasure, speared his fingers deeper and harder into her, feeling her hips begin to thrust against him.

The need to release began its long downhill roll and he knew he couldn't last long.

Then Juliette pulled him back toward the bed, his hand slipping away from her. They lay down, him on top of all her silky warm skin, and he wanted to die, right there, her naked and trembling body pressed against his.

He heard the crinkle of a condom wrapper being opened and then her fingers were back on him, a delicious torment, a glorious tease.

The condom was on and she pushed him onto his back, sliding one of those long tall legs over him. She reared up, holding him still, upright, notching the head of his penis to that damp heat. He held his breath, and she paused. Her smile wicked, she shifted, the head of his penis bumped her clitoris and slid along her. She did it again. The tease. The beautiful sexy tease. Blood pounded through his body, his penis straining against her hand.

"You want to play games?" he asked.

"I just want to play," she said, her smile both young and

seductive at the same time. They could play, he thought, all damn night. But right now, he could barely see straight.

"Jules," he whispered, so close to the edge it was killing him.

She paused and he tried to smile, but this was Juliette and he'd wanted her his whole life. And he knew she could see it on his face, how much he was feeling, and he couldn't be bothered to hide it.

"Please."

She blinked, her smile fading, her breasts rising faster with her breath.

Gorgeous, he thought, transfixed by the fire of her eyes.

Juliette sat down hard, his penis spearing into the tight heat and he cried out, his hands curling into the quilt.

He arched, lifting his hips, and she gasped, tossing her hair back.

"It's so *good,*" she breathed, finding a rhythm that made him see stars. "Always so good."

He'd wanted her so long, missed her so much, that he knew there was no way he could take this pleasure and make it last. He sat up, crushing her body to his, his lips against her breasts. He sucked her nipples, urging her harder, faster, wanting her to be as wild as him. Her fingers dug into his scalp, holding him to her.

"Yes," she breathed, and rocked hard against him, pushing him higher. He slid a hand around her back and then up over her shoulder, baring her down against him while he thrust up and forward until he was so deep inside of her there was no way he could ever leave.

Her nails bit into his back and her hips pistoned back and forth, short and sharp, and that need to release slammed into him. He clenched his jaw and stole one hand between them, his thumb finding the ridge of her clitoris and he held it there, letting her ride it out on him. Use him.

She bucked against him, kissing his neck, licking his ear, her hot breath a brand against his skin.

She lost her grace and became mindless, nearly awkward, as he felt her orgasm building. Her skin turned red as every muscle went fiercely taut.

Finally. Finally.

He bent his head to her breast and cried out, arching and shaking and shuddering against her.

He rolled to his side, taking her with him, not willing to let an inch of air come between them. He faced the ceiling, his throat thick and full of impossible emotion. It was too soon, he tried to tell himself.

Don't be an idiot. Don't ruin this moment.

But the words wouldn't stay buried. Like untrained dogs, they ran out of control.

"I love you," he said, and she jerked in surprise.

"What?" she breathed, lifting herself up to her elbow, her gorgeous hair curling over his chest.

"I love you." His smile was sweet. Tender. "I've always loved you and I always will." She only stared at him, and that wasn't entirely what he wanted, but he was down this road.

"I think I've only shown you the worst of myself," he said. "And I really want a chance to show you the best. Because you make me feel like a better man, like there are things I have to offer. To you."

"You already—"

He shook his head. "I'm not talking about sex."

"Neither am I."

"I understand if you haven't forgiven me, or even if you can't. Because I hurt you—I hurt you more than anyone should be hurt."

"I forgive you," she said.

He shook his head, unable to believe her. "You can't. Not yet."

"Do not tell me how I should feel, Tyler. That's what got us into this mess last time." She brushed the hair back from his forehead, her fingers framing his face.

"I've missed you," she said. "I feel like I've been sleeping for years and now I'm awake, and it feels so good. I don't want to go back." Her eyes were liquid and huge in the moonlight. "I don't want to go back to missing you."

"I'm right here," he said, pulling her closer. He was getting hard again and he shifted, sliding into her, making her gasp. "And I'm not going anywhere."

TWO HOURS LATER, TYLER PULLED a sheet up over Juliette's back as she slept face-first in her pillow. He smiled, trailing a finger across her skin. She slept like she did everything—wholeheartedly.

One of the many things he loved about her.

He loved her.

Watching her, his heart so big it felt as though it might beat right out of his chest, he loved her so much it hurt.

He set the box of Girl Scout cookies he'd grabbed from his car on her bedside table along with a note that she should call him as soon as she woke up.

According to his watch, he had about five hours before a morning meeting with some roofing suppliers for the build. Juliette sighed and shifted in her sleep, rolling slightly to reveal her breasts.

Man, responsibility really sucked.

"Tyler?" she whispered. "What are you doing?"

"I need to go," he said. "I have a meeting in a few hours. I should maybe get a few minutes of sleep."

She pulled hair out of her eyes and pouted. "You want to sleep?" she asked, twisting in the sheets. "Really?"

It required no thought.

"No," he said, and threw off his clothes.

AN HOUR LATER HE OPENED the door and his father's laugh boomed through the empty foyer. Another voice, mumbled and quieter, joined in, and the short hairs on the back of Tyler's neck stirred from their sex-induced slumber.

No way, he thought. *No freaking way.*

He found them in the kitchen. Richard and Miguel, sitting at the table, cards in their hands, as if it was all no big deal. As if they'd been doing it every night he went out to Remy's.

Little clues started coming together and it occurred to him that they probably had.

"When you've got a queen in the flop—" his father was saying, as if he was some kind of gambling professor.

"What the hell are you doing?" Tyler demanded.

Miguel had the good sense to put down the cards and look ashamed. But not Dad. No, not Richard Bonavie.

"Hey, son, come on in. We're just playing a little Texas hold 'em."

"I can see what you're doing," Tyler spat.

"Don't be mad at your dad," Miguel said, standing up. "It was my idea."

"I told you I wasn't going to teach you cards!" Tyler said.

"And you're not." Richard stepped in, all smiles. Tyler's hands clenched and he nearly embraced the overwhelming desire to smash his father's nose. "I am."

Tyler had to look away, take a step back. A deep breath.

Do not punch your father. Do not punch your father.

"I wanted something more for you," Tyler said, turning to Miguel. "I wanted you to have some skills. Something besides cards."

"I know," Miguel said, looking at his shoes.

"Clearly you don't!"

"Hey," Richard said. He stood and clapped a hand on Tyler's shoulder, which Tyler threw off with so much force Richard was knocked back slightly.

"I don't understand what the big deal is!" Richard said.

"You never do, Dad!" he yelled. "You don't see the big deal about walking away from your family. You don't see the big deal about mooching off your son. About vanishing for months at a time. About credit-card fraud—"

"I told you I had nothing to do with that," Richard said, his chin suddenly hard, as though his pride had been offended.

"Did Miguel tell you that I didn't want him to learn how to play cards?"

"Yeah, but—"

"And you did it anyway?"

Richard's eyes narrowed. "Last I checked, *I* was *your* father. Not the other way around."

Tyler laughed. He laughed so hard it hurt. It hurt from his toes to his heart, his gut and his throat. His father was never going to understand what was wrong. Never.

"Get out of my house," he said.

Miguel crouched to grab his coat. "I'm sorry, Tyler. I am. It's not—"

"Not you," Tyler said, stopping the boy. This moment had been a long time coming, years and years of pretending that what passed between them was working. Was worth it.

Tyler pointed at his father. "Get out of my house."

CHAPTER SIXTEEN

"YOU'RE KICKING ME OUT? This isn't even your house."

"It's more mine than yours," he said. "And I want you to leave."

For a second Richard looked at a loss and Tyler felt a moment's pity. But then he laughed again, the sound colored with desperation.

"Good one, son. You nearly had me going there." Richard crouched in front of the kitchen liquor cabinet to pull out a bottle of Jack. "Come on, why don't we all have a drink and—"

Tyler slammed the door shut and had to force himself not to do more. Not to do worse. Years of letting this man steer him into waters he had no desire to visit—waters he thought he deserved because of his blood, because of the people he'd hurt and left behind. All those years coalesced into something so dark, so damning, he couldn't turn away from this path.

His anger wouldn't let him.

"I'm done with you, Dad."

"Ty, come on."

Just then, Richard looked every moment of his age, his belly curving over the edge of his belt, silver chest hair fighting its way out of his collar. A con man at the end of his days, and Tyler could see where the old man would end up. Some bachelor apartment off the strip with sagging furniture and water stains on the ceiling, waiting for his luck to turn around.

Tyler felt bad, he truly did, but he didn't want to end up there with him.

And Richard would have no second thoughts about dragging Tyler down to his level.

"Pack your stuff," he said to Richard's stunned face.

"You'll regret this," Richard said, finally stumbling into action.

"I won't," Tyler said, thinking of Juliette. Of what his life could be without Richard around his neck like a stone. Something in him was swimming toward the surface, pulling him toward a future that had no Richard in it, and he was happy. Hopeful.

"I'm sorry, Dad. I am. But you have to go."

Tyler followed his father into the living room, where Richard had been keeping his stuff.

"Don't come looking for me when your money runs out," Richard said, tossing golf shirts into his bag.

Tyler felt a twinge of guilt and pulled out his wallet. "How much do you need, Dad?"

Richard spun around. "I won't take a penny of your—"

"You have no cash, Dad. You can't even get a bus ticket." He unfolded some bills, enough for a bus to New Orleans and a first-class ticket to Las Vegas.

"You don't know what I have," Richard said, his voice mean and snide. Richard Bonavie with his back against the wall—Tyler had seen it a million times.

He pressed the money into his dad's fist and when Richard looked as if he was going to toss it in Tyler's face, he closed his fist around his father's as hard as he could, putting every empty moment they'd spent together into his grip.

Pain bracketed Richard's lips but he said nothing.

"This is the last money you'll see from me," Tyler said.

Cowed, Richard took it.

Tyler watched, his heart hard, thoughts of Juliette a bright light guiding him to safer waters.

Tyler opened the door for his father, the night and the unknown and the next big con waiting for Richard like an old lover.

Richard paused at the threshold. "I tried," he whispered. "I know you don't believe that, but I did the best I could."

Tyler did believe it, and for a moment he felt this resolve waiver. He felt like he was kicking a puppy that didn't know any better.

"But the kid is good," his father whispered. "The three of us, we could—"

"Go," Tyler said. "Just go."

He watched his father walk off into the night, toward town and the bus station, and wondered if this was how snakes felt when they got rid of that skin.

He felt new. Fresh. Capable of anything.

"I'm sorry, Tyler," Miguel whispered. "I came to him with the idea."

"It's okay," he said, watching his father walk away.

"He was pretty decent to me," Miguel said. "He didn't drink when I was here."

There was nothing to say to that. Tyler felt regret bite hard into his throat, not that he'd kicked his father out, but that his father couldn't manage to string those moments of decency together. That he couldn't rise above the worst of himself.

"He taught me a lot about cards," Miguel said.

"But cards are nothing to pin a future on, do you get that?"

"But the money—"

"Money runs out, Miguel," Tyler said. "When I found my dad ten years ago, he had so much money he couldn't spend it fast enough. But he did. Look at him."

Miguel looked out into the night. Richard, once the big man, was walking away with borrowed money in his pocket, about to take a bus.

"You're starting this job after school in a week," Tyler said. "A real job. And I bet in time, you'll be a foreman on that job. And you'll have skills you can take anywhere. You'll have a way to take care of your sister for good, not just for a while."

Miguel licked his lips and nodded. "I guess," he said.

"You guess?" Tyler laughed. "I think it's a whole lot better than I guess, considering you tried to steal Suzy."

Miguel rolled his eyes. "Dude! You are so weird."

"Keep that up and I won't teach you how to drive her."

"Did I say weird?" Miguel asked. "I meant awesome."

"I know you did, kid. I know you did."

SUNDAY MORNING, Juliette stood on The Manor's brand-new front porch and took a deep breath. Another one. She smoothed a hand down the front of her blue skirt, wishing she'd taken the time to iron it a little better.

Her hands, slippery with sweat, were in danger of dropping the box she carried, so before she could delay and grow any more nervous she reached out and rang the doorbell.

She was here to show Tyler and herself—and Priscilla, if the old lady cared—that she was ready to love all of

Tyler. Even the bad stuff. And that meant getting to know his father.

The door swung open, revealing Tyler holding a steaming cup of coffee. A long slow smile that was better than a kiss crossed his face.

"Well, now," he said, leaning against the door and making her want to giggle with nerves and lust. "To what do I owe this honor?"

"Here," she said, thrusting the small white box at him. Nerves made her awkward, ungracious.

"What's this?" he asked.

"Muffins."

"You baked?"

She snorted and then tried very hard to pretend she hadn't. "No. Don't be ridiculous."

"I wasn't," he said, stepping aside so she could walk in. "I was being hopeful. Juliette Tremblant at my door in a skirt carrying muffins? Where's the porno music?"

She laughed, helpless against this man's humor. His charm. This was why she loved him, because he brought light to her darkest days, turned her gray life into Technicolor.

"I'm here to meet your father," she said, turning to face him in time to see his expression go hard. Cold. "Is that a problem?"

"I'm guessing by the skirt and muffins you're not here as police chief?"

She shook her head. "I want to know all of you, Tyler," she said. "Good, bad and otherwise. And that means your father."

Tyler put down the mug and box on the table in the foyer and stepped close to Juliette, his warmth embracing her, his smell enveloping her.

"I hate to disappoint you," he said, his fingers toying

with the hem of the gauzy white shirt she wore. Desire seeped into her and she watched his fingers unbutton the bottom button. And the next one up. "Since you're all dressed up in your Sunday best, bringing gifts, but I kicked him out Friday night."

"What?" she asked, rallying her brain function. "Why?"

His fingers kept climbing the buttons on her shirt, until he slipped it off her shoulders, revealing a thin camisole.

"Can I tell you later?" he asked, kissing her shoulder, her collarbone. "I get so turned on by a woman bearing baked goods."

An hour later, wrapped in the old worn wedding-ring-patterned quilt that Tyler had had on his bed since high school, Juliette sat facing him. Sunlight poured in the room and across Tyler's face, illuminating the day-old beard, the dark circles under his eyes. She hadn't noticed the other night how thin he'd gotten. He was all planes and angles.

He was working too hard, which, frankly, was not something Juliette ever thought she'd say about him.

"These are great," he said, finishing off his third muffin.

"I'll be sure to tell Cindy down at The Sunrise." She picked the last blueberry out of hers and handed the rest of it to Tyler. Suddenly, she wanted to take care of him. Make sure he slept. Was fed. The boy needed a keeper. "You want to tell me about your father?"

"Not really."

"Please, Ty. No more secrets."

He glanced heavenward and then brushed off his hands and sat up against the headboard, the sheet pooling low on his hips.

She kept her eyes on his face, refusing to be distracted by the muscles ribbing his stomach. The bite mark on his neck.

"Why'd you kick him out, Ty?"

"Don't get mad," he said.

"Uh-oh."

"Friday night, I came home from your house and found Miguel here. Richard was teaching him how to play cards."

"What?"

"From what I gathered, Miguel left his backpack here one night when I was gone, and when he came here to pick it up he found Dad, bored and willing to teach him how to play cards."

Tyler told her about how Miguel had first approached Tyler to teach him, but how instead, he'd put Miguel to work cleaning up the house.

"That little sneak," she said.

"Right, well. It was time for Dad to go, and that just gave me an excuse to make it happen."

"Was your father here looking for the gems?" she asked, and Tyler's eyes sharpened.

"Why would you think that?"

She blinked. "Why wouldn't I? Your mother broke into the house twice because she was convinced they were here."

"Dad didn't find any gems," he finally said, pulling the sheet up higher on his lap.

"I don't hold your parents' sins against you," she said, wondering why he looked so uncomfortable.

"That's a relief," he said, his voice snide. "I've got enough of my own."

This was not going the way she had hoped. She was just

trying to get some answers and he was acting as if he was hiding something.

"Did you know your parents were involved in the gem theft seven years ago?"

"Are you interrogating me?" he asked, and she sat back, wounded by his tone.

"No," she said, but inwardly she winced. Maybe she was. A little. "Why would you—"

"Because you're the police chief," he said. "And my parents are crooks."

"I'm just trying to figure out why everyone thinks the gems are here."

"I didn't know. I was living in Vegas at the time but...I was occupied."

"With what?"

"A performer with Cirque du Soleil."

Oh. She tried not to be jealous, but she couldn't help it, and his attitude wasn't helping.

She'd come here, damn it, to show him she was serious. That she was ready to put aside the past and their differences and try to make it work. And he was treating her as though she was the bad guy.

Angry, she stood, dropping the quilt and pulling on her skirt and tank top. "You know, I'm your sister's best friend," she snapped. "And I was looking after this house before you came along as a favor to Margot, who is like family to me."

"I know," he muttered, reaching out for her hand, but she slapped it away.

"I just want to help, Tyler, that's all. I'm not the enemy. And I won't be treated like I am."

"I'm sorry," he said. "I am."

She shook back her hair, watching him carefully, the difference between them suddenly seeming bigger than ever.

TYLER'S HEART WAS POUNDING right out of his chest. "Please," he said. "Talking about my parents isn't…isn't something I enjoy. And I hate that Margot and Savannah and Katie—" *and now me,* he thought "—are all caught up in this gem nightmare. I'm sorry. I am."

She appeared to be wavering, so he did what any desperate, hot-blooded man hiding a fortune in gems from his police chief lover would do—he pulled ever so slowly on her arm, trying to get her back in bed.

"I'm not a fish," she snapped. "You can't reel me in." But she didn't pull her hand away and she took one step and then another closer to the bed.

"I've been alone a long time, Jules," he said. "The only people who held me accountable to anything had lower standards than I did. It's going to take me a while to get used to being a good guy."

"Don't make a fool of me, Tyler," she said, and then without any more resistance, she put one knee on the bed and leaned over to kiss him.

She spent the rest of the day at The Manor, much to Tyler's delight. He made her eggs and after the sun set he tried to convince her to stay for pizza, but she resisted.

"I have to go," she said at the door, a totally different woman than the one who'd arrived that morning. Chief Tremblant, without all the starch. "I need to get ready for work tomorrow."

"I'll call you," he said as she stepped across the new porch and into the twilight. She turned, the breeze toying with her hair, and blew him a kiss.

Once she was gone, Tyler shut the door and nearly ran through the house back to his room. He was going to take that damn diamond out to Remy's and toss it into the swamp.

He wasn't going to have his life fall down around him

for some mistake one of his parents made. No way. Not when he had so much to lose.

He yanked the zipper down on the side pocket of his leather duffel and tossed out the top two socks, looking for the black pair he'd hidden behind them.

The socks weren't there.

Trying to keep his cool, he opened the main pocket and dug through shirts and underwear, a couple of pairs of jeans, until he found one black sock at the bottom.

He tore apart the bag. His room. He ran into the room Richard had been staying in, but it was empty.

No socks. No diamond.

The gem was gone.

And in his mind it was no coincidence that his father happened to be gone, too.

Swearing, he found his cell phone and dialed his brother's number.

"Carter O'Neill," his brother said after the first ring. Carter was always Johnny-on-the-spot when it came to his cell phone.

"Carter." Tyler rested his head against the doorjamb, feeling worse than he had in a long time. He hated calling his big brother for help, like some kind of child, but there was no one else he could talk to. Not even Juliette, despite what she might say. She was police, and this was a very nonpolice matter. "We have a problem," Tyler said, and launched into the whole story.

"You're sure Dad has it?" Carter asked when Tyler was done.

"It's a pretty big coincidence, isn't it? A diamond is missing and so is a confessed jewel thief."

"I'm just saying, you put it in a sock, Tyler. Is there any way you've lost—"

"No!" Tyler yelled, in no mood to be baby-brothered by

Carter. Despite the fact that putting a diamond in a sock was a dumb move, especially since he and Dad swapped clothes like girls. "There's no way."

Carter sighed and Tyler burned, recognizing that sigh from a dozen other phone conversations when Tyler had reached out for help.

"Forget it," Tyler said. "The damn thing is gone, it doesn't matter anymore."

A big gong was struck in his head.

It truly didn't matter anymore.

With the diamond off O'Neill property, it was no longer his problem. And considering that Richard had been a person of interest when the gems initially disappeared, if he was stupid enough to get caught with the diamond now, it was pretty cut-and-dried.

Savannah and Margot wouldn't be implicated.

Juliette wouldn't be forced to get involved.

Everything was going to be okay.

"Doesn't matter?" Carter asked. "If Dad gets caught, it will be all over the papers."

"So?" He'd been all over the papers before; it only hurt for a minute.

"So, some of us have careers, Tyler. Careers that hinge on keeping this kind of garbage out of the papers."

Carter was mayor pro-temp of Baton Rouge, and Tyler had to admit that if Dad got caught with this gem, it would be ugly for Carter.

Sympathy flooded Tyler. Just as his problems got better, Carter's got worse. O'Neills could not catch a break.

"I'll see if I can get ahold of Dad," Tyler said.

"Do that," Carter snapped. "I'll see what I can find out."

Carter hung up and Tyler dialed his father's cell phone number, but the line never rang, which meant Dad had lost his phone—again—and it was sitting someplace with a dead battery.

Or Dad had ditched the phone, not wanting to be found.

And Tyler, a selfish, disloyal brother—was glad.

CHAPTER SEVENTEEN

AS FAR AS WEEKS WENT, Tyler thought, this was one for the books. Perhaps, he thought, leaving his meeting with Derek and some volunteer builders, the best week ever.

Dad hadn't surfaced, but then neither had the diamond. And while that was sending Carter into a tizzy, Tyler felt better than he had in years, as though he was stepping out into the sun for the first time.

He started Suzy and pulled out his cell phone, pressing redial to get Juliette.

"Chief Tremblant," she said, and he smiled, pulling out of Remy's parking lot where he'd held his meeting.

"That is seriously the sexiest thing I've ever heard," he said.

"You didn't think that when it was my father!"

"Ugh!" He grimaced and shook his head, trying hard to dislodge that mental image. "Come on, Jules. Don't be sick."

She laughed, the sound like fine wine. "How was the meeting?"

"Awesome. We should be ready to go on Monday. How about you?"

"Well—" she sighed "—I've got my home visit meeting scheduled for next week. I need to clean out my home office, get stuff organized for kids." She paused. "Do you know what kids need?"

"Let's talk about it over dinner," he said, looking at

the sinking sun on the horizon as he drove through town. "Ben Cruise owns that new fancy place on Main Street, and he's one of the volunteers. He invited me to come out anytime."

"That sounds great. Why don't you give me another hour?" she said. "There are a few things I need to do first. Do kids like bunk beds?"

"Five-year-olds, yeah. Not Miguel." He shook his head, smiling. She was excited and Juliette would be a fantastic foster parent, but every once in a while, he was very glad to be around to help.

They hung up and after he parked Suzy, he climbed the steps of his porch by two, humming "Feel Like Making Love" under his breath.

But the song died in his throat when he saw the front door hanging open.

He'd gotten lax over the past few weeks with the alarm and locking the door, but he was pretty sure he'd closed it that morning.

Dad, he thought, heavy anger settling in his stomach like rocks.

The door eased open under the pressure of his fist, but as he turned the corner into the living room, it wasn't his dad sitting on the couch.

"Miguel?" Tyler asked.

"The front door wasn't locked," Miguel said, looking manic. His hands shook, and his eyes were way past dilated. If he didn't know better, Tyler would think the kid was on something. And Louisa…Louisa sat in the shadows of the couch looking like a stray cat.

The air smelled like fear. And blood.

"You okay?" he asked, foreboding blossoming in his brain.

"We need money," Miguel said, leaping off the couch. Louisa flinched. "Right now."

Tyler approached Miguel like the boy was a wild dog. "Please, Miguel. You need to calm down—"

"Don't tell me what I need to do!" Miguel yelled. "You have no clue!"

"Okay." Tyler nodded. "Then why don't you tell me. Why don't you sit down—" He reached out to touch Miguel, to guide him back toward the couch, and Louisa leaped up.

"Don't touch him!" she screamed, flying around Miguel to smack at Tyler's legs. She got Tyler good in the crotch and he swore, trying to protect himself and calm Louisa down. Her braids flew wild around her face and Miguel grabbed his sister with shaking hands and pushed her back behind him.

But not fast enough.

Tyler got a good look at Louisa's face.

Her poor, battered face.

"Oh, my God," Tyler breathed, bile rising in his throat. "What happened?"

Miguel shook his head, his eyes diamond bright and just as hard. "I just need money, Tyler. So we can leave."

"I can give you money. I can help, Miguel. I swear I can. But you have to tell me what's going on."

Miguel held out hands balled tightly into fists. He turned them over and opened his palms.

It took Tyler a second to register what Miguel was showing him.

"Is that Louisa's blood?" Tyler asked, surprised his voice was so calm and heavy, when inside he felt as if all the walls were coming down. Fury, sympathy, fear and worry rolled through him, tearing him apart.

Miguel shook his head, holding himself so still Tyler

worried the boy was going to break before he bent. Miguel's shoulders shook. Tears flooded his eyes and poured down his face. Tyler reached for him, but Miguel collapsed back onto the couch and Louisa climbed into his lap, holding on to him while he sobbed, his entire body rocking.

"Miguel?" Tyler asked, bending his knees so he could look right into Miguel's eyes. "Whose blood is that?"

"I killed him," Miguel breathed. "I killed my dad."

JULIETTE LEFT HER OFFICE, waving good-night to Owens, who was surly because he was on dispatch, and headed out the front door to her car and the night and Tyler.

Honestly, she didn't realize how unhappy she'd been before this week. And she hated to think of what would have become of her if Tyler hadn't come crashing back into her life. What kind of dried up, humorless woman she would have turned into.

She paused at the curb to the parking lot.

Her father leaned against her car.

It had been weeks since they'd spoken, and her father's smile tore at her heart.

Daddy, she thought. *I missed you.* It surprised her, but she did. Perhaps it was all the love in the air, but she wished she and Dad could go back to the way things used to be. Before she was chief, back when the job wasn't between them.

"Hello, Juliette," he said.

"Dad?" she said, noticing how much weight he'd lost, how ashen his cheeks were. He wasn't taking care of himself. "Are you okay?" she asked.

"I'm fine," he said, waving off her concern. "Have you seen the news?" he asked.

"What news?" she asked, stepping off the curb. She unlocked her car, opened the rear door and put her briefcase inside.

Her phone rang and she checked the display. Tyler.

Dad's hand touched her shoulder. "Before you answer that, I need to talk to you," he said, his eyes level and serious. "I'm asking you for just a few minutes of your time. As a police chief."

She sighed and then turned off the phone. Tyler probably just wanted to tell her about dinner plans.

Or talk dirty.

It was a toss-up.

"Okay, Dad," she said, slipping her phone in her pocket. "Shoot."

"It's about Tyler's father—"

"Are you kidding me?" she asked. "We haven't spoken in weeks and this is—"

"He was arrested in Los Angeles. He had the Pacific Diamond in his possession."

TYLER SAT ON THE FLOOR, watching the two demolished kids on his couch clutching at each other just to stay afloat. He tried to prioritize, slot the different terrible aspects of Miguel's story into manageable holes. Things that needed to be dealt with.

Louisa didn't seem to have anything more than a black eye and a fat lip, so the hospital could wait.

"You think Ramon is dead?" Tyler asked after Miguel managed to get out the whole nightmarish story. Dead bodies seemed like they should be step one.

"I hit him really hard. The bottle broke everywhere," Miguel whispered, his eyes on Louisa, who was beginning to doze against her brother. It was getting late and the little girl had been through so much. "But it's not like I stuck around to check."

"You were protecting your sister," Tyler said, putting his hand on Miguel's shoulder. Miguel's eyes closed, tears streaming down his cheeks. "You did what any good big brother would do. Do you hear me, Miguel?"

Miguel nodded, stroking his sister's hands with his bloody fingers.

Tyler didn't know how his heart could hurt more, how he could look at this brave and scared boy and love him any more than he did.

He wanted to sweep both of these kids up in his arms, keep them safe.

"I'm going to take care of this," he said, and stood.

He dug his cell phone out of his pocket and called Juliette—she would know what to do. But her message clicked on and he couldn't quite believe it.

"Call me," he said. "It's urgent."

He tried the station next, asking the man who answered the phone if Juliette was still there.

"She left about ten minutes ago," he said, which meant that Juliette had to be at home. He didn't have that number. How stupid was that?

Phone book, he needed a phone book.

He pulled open the first drawer in the kitchen just as thunderous knocking on his front door rattled the windows.

"Open up!" a man yelled. "Police!"

He heard Miguel scramble in the living room and he raced down the hall.

"Calm down," he said to the totally freaked out boy, though his own nerves were about to snap. "Take your sister and go upstairs."

"What are you going to do?" Miguel asked, helping his sister to her feet.

"Don't worry," he said, because he wasn't all that sure. "I'll think of something."

The kids headed upstairs and there was more knocking, this time accompanied by muffled Spanish.

Tyler lifted the lace curtain in the living room a fraction of an inch and caught a glimpse of the men on the porch.

Owens. Great.

And Ramon, holding a bath towel to his head.

At least he wasn't dead, but Tyler was inflated by a bright red and burning hot need to spill more of that man's blood. To take every pain Ramon had inflicted on his children and return it—doubled—upon him.

Tyler dug his wallet from his back pocket and flipped it open, flinging cards on the floor until he found what he wanted.

He sent a quick prayer heavenward and called in the cavalry—Nora Sullivan.

Luckily, she was working late and once she was filled in on the situation, she was practically out the door.

"Just keep Ramon away from those kids. Do whatever you need to, but keep those kids away from their father and out of jail."

With his orders in mind and the kids safely upstairs, Tyler tossed open the front door, sickened by the men that stood there.

"Owens," he said with a sneer. "Can I ask why you're fouling up my brand-new porch?"

"Watch it, Tyler," Owens said, hooking a thumb between his gut and his gun belt. "We're here on police business."

"Where are my kids?" Ramon shouted, his wide, dark face streaked with blood, his eyes poisoned with anger.

Tyler clenched his fists, trying to keep himself under control, trying to stall for time so Nora could get here.

"They're not here," he said, and stepped back to slam the door, but Owens quickly got a foot in the door.

"Hold on a second, Tyler. I got some questions—"

"I know they're in there!" Ramon shouted. "Miguel spends more time here than he does at home. You're trying to steal my kids—"

"Steal!" Tyler cried. "Like you care, you drunk son of a bitch—"

"Hey now," Owens said, holding up a hand, but Ramon tossed aside the bloody towel and charged Tyler, who met the man with a joyful heart and a serious right hook.

Ramon stumbled and Tyler launched himself forward, knocking the man to the ground. His veins humming with bloodlust, Tyler straddled the man and punched him, feeling the cartilage in Roman's nose go to mush, sending blood spraying across the white porch.

Owens tried to get involved but Tyler shoved the police officer back.

Tyler lifted Ramon by the neck of his shirt, his head listing sideways, covered in old and fresh blood. "You don't deserve those kids. You don't—"

Owens's fist came out of nowhere, catching Tyler in the eye and he toppled sideways before being yanked to his knees by his own neck, which Owens had wrapped his arm around.

"You just don't know when to quit, do you?" Owens asked, squeezing even harder until Tyler saw stars. "Now I gotta take you down to the station."

Owens called in help to take Ramon to the clinic and Tyler waited in the back of the squad car. He hoped, prayed that with Tyler in the backseat of his squad car, Owens would lose interest in the kids.

"I'm going to check the house," Owens told the other officer, "see if those kids are here."

Crap.

With nothing else at his disposal, Tyler went ape shit. Screaming, spitting, kicking at the window, anything to get Owens back to the car and away from the house.

He didn't want those kids taken away in a squad car. He didn't want them held in a cell when their night had been horrific enough. He wanted them at The Manor until someone who loved them could find them.

"Don't make me taze you!" Owens said, sliding into the front seat.

He started up the car and Tyler watched the window of his upstairs bedroom, where Miguel stood.

"Stay," he mouthed to Miguel. "Stay right there."

JULIETTE STOOD IN HER DARK living room, surrounded by the glow of her television, and felt the world go sideways. It took five minutes for the story to come back around, but there it was. Richard Bonavie being led away from the Los Angeles airport in cuffs, illuminated by a hundred flashbulbs.

"Richard Bonavie was found with the thirty-karat Pacific Diamond that was stolen from the Bellagio Ancient Treasures Exhibit seven years ago. Bonavie was initially a person of interest in the crime but was released due to insufficient evidence. Bonavie is now being transferred to Nevada for questioning."

"Tyler was in Las Vegas at that time, wasn't he?" her dad asked.

"He doesn't know anything about it," she snapped, though as the words came out of her mouth she knew she was lying. He might not have known about the gems seven years ago, but he sure as hell knew about them now.

It was just too much of a coincidence that Richard left

The Manor a week ago, and now he gets arrested with a gem that had been missing for years.

Maybe Tyler didn't know Richard found the gem, she told herself, trying to put the brakes on her anger. He said he didn't, and maybe he was telling the truth.

If you love him, you'll go with that. At least until proven otherwise.

But she had a bad feeling she was going to be proven otherwise.

She reached into her pocket and turned on her phone, which immediately began ringing.

She didn't check the caller ID, sure of who it was.

"Tyler," she said, "what the hell is going on?"

"This isn't Tyler," Officer Kavanaugh said, and something in his voice turned Juliette's blood to ice.

"What's wrong?"

"Well," he said, huffing a deep sigh. "I figured you'd want to know, we've got Tyler O'Neill in a holding cell with a black eye and Owens is filling out paperwork charging Tyler with assaulting an officer."

Holy. Shit.

"That's not all. Ramon Pastor is at the clinic, with a broken nose and about twenty stitches in his head."

"Where's Miguel?"

"No one knows."

"I'll be right there," she said. She hung up and headed for the door.

"Everything okay?" her dad asked.

"No," she said bluntly, standing at the door. Her whole world was falling down around her and she didn't know where to begin. Find Miguel? Talk to Tyler? Deal with Owens?

She put her hand against the wall for just a moment,

feeling as though her knees might buckle under the weight of everything that was going wrong.

"I'll come with you," her father said, turning off the TV.

"Dad, you can't get involved."

"I won't."

She snorted.

"I know I've screwed up and I'm more sorry than I can say. But I just want to be moral support. You don't have to do this alone."

Not doing it alone sounded good, and maybe she was being a coward, and quite possibly making the wrong decision, but her father was there. Sturdy and solid in a world gone liquid.

She nodded and he followed her out the door.

A few minutes later, the door into the squad room opened with a bang and Juliette stomped into the room, ready to breathe fire over her entire staff, over the entire town, for that matter. "What the hell is going on here?" she barked.

Owens, who'd clearly disobeyed her orders to stay on dispatch, made no attempt to disguise his smirk.

"Answers, Owens," she said, coming to stand right in front of him, a hairbreadth away from his sweaty face. "And I better like them, or it's your badge."

"Ramon Pastor called around 7:00 p.m., saying he'd been attacked by his son. I went to check it out—"

"Why?" she asked, propping her hands on her hips. "You're on desk duty. Furthermore, you were on dispatch."

Owens managed to look abashed. "Kavanaugh had it covered."

She glanced over at Officer Kavanaugh, whose expression said he was mad as hell to be tied up in this.

"Disobeying orders," she snapped. "This night is not going to go well for you, Owens. Keep going."

"Mr. Pastor had been hit over the head with a bottle but he said he knew where the boy was—"

"And you *took* him? You took a drunk, angry father with you to find his son? That's flagrant breach of protocol."

The snide expression slowly melted off his face, replaced by worry. "He knew where the boy was but he wouldn't tell me unless I took him."

"And you're not a good enough policeman to figure it out?" she demanded. "This whole town knows Miguel's been spending time with Tyler. You knew where Miguel would be and you took Ramon with you to watch the fireworks, didn't you? Maybe get Tyler in trouble?"

Anger seethed in her, her hands shaking with the desire to tear Owens apart.

"And what's this about assaulting an officer?" she asked.

Owens shot a dark look at Kavanaugh.

"Eyes up here!" she boomed, and Owens snapped to like a scared puppy.

"O'Neill hit me, shoved me off his porch."

"And what did you do to Tyler?" she asked. "If I go back into that cell what kind of shape will he be in?"

Owens's neck turned red and splotchy. She put her hand over the paperwork he'd been signing and crumpled it up in a ball. She tossed it, right in front of his face, into the garbage.

Her dad cleared his throat behind her and she whirled to face him.

"You got a problem with how I'm handling this?" she asked.

It took a moment but he shook his head.

"Disobeying orders and breach of protocol on top of the letters in your file are enough," she told Owens.

"For…" Owens looked over her shoulder at her father. "For what?"

"You're fired." She held out her hand. "Badge and firearm."

"I'll fight you," Owens said, fumbling as he unhooked his badge and firearm.

"Please do," she said, relishing the chance to cut this man loose.

She took his badge and firearm into her office and locked it in the top drawer of her desk, then stepped back into the squad room.

"Now," she said, "do we have any idea where Miguel and Louisa Pastor are?"

CHAPTER EIGHTEEN

KAVANAUGH SHOOK HIS HEAD.

"Owens?" The shell-shocked man stared down at the picture of his wife, but Juliette could not be moved by sympathy anymore; the man had made his own bed.

"I didn't check the house," he said. "I made sure Ramon got to the clinic and I brought Tyler here. I have no idea where the kids are."

She had a hunch that if they had been at The Manor, they'd still be there. But only one person knew that for sure—Tyler.

She wished she had more time before talking to him. Time to cool off, gather her thoughts, get her defenses in place.

But Miguel and Louisa were out there alone, and that's what mattered.

She swung open the door to the holding cells and stepped down the long yellow hallway to cell four, where Tyler sat on a bench, his long legs stretched out in front of him.

His eye going black.

He was still so handsome it hurt to look at him. Still so loved she couldn't imagine he'd actually betrayed her.

"Hello, honey," he drawled, and she stiffened at the endearment. She didn't know whether the ground she stood on was safe or was about to fall away under her feet. The kids, Tyler, the gem—nothing was a safe bet.

"You okay?" she asked, nodding at his face.

"Fine," he said. "Owens hits like a girl."

"And Ramon?"

"He came after me and I acted in self-defense." His lip curled. "No crime in enjoying it."

She imagined he did. Putting fists to Ramon was something she'd dreamed of many times.

"Where are the kids?" she asked.

"You have to trust me, Juliette," he whispered, and she couldn't control the sharp bark of laughter that erupted from her throat.

"You're kidding, right?" she asked, the anger and doubt spilling out from behind the walls she'd tried to build around them. "Trust you?"

He stood, uncurling from his place against the wall, and crossed the cell. His fingers touched hers around the bars and she jerked her hand away.

"What's happened?" he asked, ignoring her question. "Why are you—"

Suddenly, his face changed. His eyes flicked from Juliette to the doorway behind her and ferocity filled his expression.

She turned to see her father.

"Everything okay in here?" Jasper asked carefully, and for a moment, she was warmed by his concern.

"How in the world did I know you were behind this, Jasper?" Tyler asked, stepping away from the bars. "You just can't stand having me around."

"Dad has nothing to do with this," she said.

"Really?" Tyler asked, shooting her a toxic look. "I'm beaten up and thrown in jail. It seems awfully familiar." He shook his head. "Your father can't see past the fact that I'm an O'Neill. And you're listening to him!"

"*Your* father," she yelled, lunging toward the bars, "was caught at LAX with the Pacific Diamond!"

His eyes searched hers.

"It's true," she said. "It's all over the networks."

"Goddamn it," he muttered, and turned away.

Cold seeped into her, leeched from the air and the cement.

It was real. Every fear and suspicion it hurt to contemplate was accurate.

"Where'd the gem come from?" she asked.

"Does it matter?"

"Of course it matters!" she shouted. "Because if that diamond came from The Manor, it means you lied to me, Tyler. You lied to my face after swearing you wouldn't."

He didn't say anything and the silence was damning.

"What do you want me to say, Juliette?" he asked, his cheeks bright with color. "I found that damn diamond weeks ago in a box in the attic, and you know what that means?"

"That you lied!"

"It means that either my mother put it there...or Margot did."

Juliette blinked. She hadn't thought of that.

"Margot wouldn't—" she said, but Tyler interrupted.

"You don't know that. Not for sure. But you're the chief of police, so if I told you about the diamond, you'd have to bring my eighty-year-old grandmother in for questioning."

"So you lied to me to protect your family?" It hurt. It hurt because she'd pushed away all the family she had left to protect him. It hurt because she'd started to believe that she and Tyler were a family of sorts.

"And you," he said. "I wanted to keep you far away from

having to make those decisions, because I knew it would kill you."

He was right. It would have killed her. But it was her job!

"So you made the decision for me," she said. "Just like ten years ago."

Tyler threw up his hands. "Yep. You're right. I lied to protect you. To protect my family. But now Dad's going to jail, where he should have been all along."

"Should have been all along?" she asked. "What do you mean?"

Tyler stilled. "He stole the gems in the first place. Let his partner, Joel Woods, take the fall."

"Oh, my God," she breathed, backing up a step. And then another. "Why wasn't...how did he..."

"Dad was questioned but released because he wasn't at the drop-off when the cops arrived. There was no evidence."

"But he told you?"

Tyler nodded.

"And you failed to tell me that your father was a confessed jewel thief?"

Eventually, slowly, Tyler nodded again.

She was breathless, weak with hurt.

"We said no lies," she whispered. "And you still didn't tell me."

Tyler just nodded, his arms hanging at his sides as if broken.

A haze filled her head and she could barely see through it, much less think.

"Don't you have anything to say?" she asked, wishing there was something he could say that would make it all right but knowing there wasn't.

"I can explain," he said. "But not here. Not—" He

nodded toward Jasper. "You have to trust me, Juliette. Please."

This wasn't sex. This wasn't a boy in trouble. This was her heart. Again. And he'd managed to find the old wounds and reopen them.

He'd lied, to her face, over and over again. Before they'd slept together, she could almost understand it. But after… the hurt was so deep, so painful, it made her numb.

"I can't," she said. "You're the same, Tyler O'Neill. And I was an idiot to think you'd changed."

She started to walk away.

"And you have?" he asked, his voice sharp and tipped in poison. "You said you forgave me, but the second something goes wrong you're walking away with your dad."

She ignored the truth in his words, too hurt to contemplate the things she was doing wrong.

Instead she turned. "Have you called your lawyer?"

"You can't be serious. What am I being charged with?"

"You can have one more phone call," she said, and left, Tyler's curses ringing in her ears.

He wasn't being charged with anything, but he didn't know that.

She was in the parking lot before she realized her father had followed her.

Her feet dragged to a halt but she didn't turn. She wouldn't show her father her tears so he could mock her, tell her he'd told her so.

"You're loving this, aren't you?" she whispered. "You're right and I'm wrong. And now it can go back to just being you and me. Alone. Forever."

"That's not what I wanted, Juliette," he said. His steps came closer and she held up her hand, making it very clear she wasn't in the mood for a fatherly hug.

"A man like—"

"Don't, Dad."

"Listen to me," he said, putting his hand on her shoulder despite her no-touch signal. "A man like that will do anything to protect the people he loves. He'll lie to them, manipulate them. He'll walk away from them."

She turned disbelieving eyes on him. "You're defending Tyler O'Neill?"

"No," he said, shaking his head. He dropped his hands, holding them awkwardly at his sides as if he knew they should be full or useful and was surprised that they weren't.

For a moment she saw him as a man without. A man without his beloved wife, without the career that defined him, without the love and affection of his daughter.

Dad was a man alone, and in a night full of heartbreak, it seemed like the last straw. She wished she could feel something other than her bleeding and broken heart. Sympathy, or something, but Tyler's betrayal stole everything out of her, leaving her raw.

She had to force herself to forget about Tyler, starting right now. Pull every memory out at the root until he didn't exist for her.

"I'm not defending him," Dad said, "because what he did was wrong. But I'm telling you I understand what he did. And why."

It was too much.

"I'm done being lied to and manipulated by the men in my life," she snapped. "I deserve better. I deserve to be treated like a woman who can make her own decisions. I don't need protection—I don't need someone watching my every move."

Jasper nodded, his eyes glittering.

"I don't forgive you for what you've done," she said.

"I know."

"I need to go find Miguel," she said, and her dad nodded as if accepting that she had nothing to give him and somehow that was the saddest thing of all.

"You did a good job back there," he said. "With Owens. Letting Tyler cool his heels made sense, too."

He lifted his hand in a meager wave and then walked away to his car.

Repairing bridges with her father would have to wait. She grabbed her cell phone and called Miguel but didn't get an answer.

She called Patricia next, but she hadn't seen the kids, either.

She drove out to The Manor, but it was dark and empty.

Finally, she called Nora to let her know what was going on.

"Nora," Juliette said when the counselor answered the phone. "We've got a situation with Miguel and Louisa—"

"I know," Nora said. "We're in the emergency room in Ellicott City."

"We?"

"I've got the kids. Tyler called me when he couldn't find you."

How many times, she wondered, could her world get rearranged? How many times could she be left sorting through Tyler O'Neill's truths and lies, measuring the good he did against the destructive?

"I'll be right there," she said, and hung up.

HOURS LATER, TYLER WATCHED his brother blow into the holding cells like a cyclone. Contained, beautiful in a way, but capable of massive destruction.

"Well, well," Carter said, stopping in front of the bars Tyler stood behind. His suit was perfect. Hair—perfect. His face looked like it belonged in profile on a coin somewhere.

Carter was like royalty. If the Notorious O'Neills had such a thing.

"Tyler in jail." Carter glanced around the yellow walls and bars as if he could smell them and it wasn't good. "Again."

"Hope I didn't bother you," Tyler drawled, and Carter's eyebrows arched. Tyler wanted a fight. He needed to tear things apart, throw things against the wall and obliterate everything in his path.

Luckily, Carter was always good for a fight. Tyler just needed his brother to get him out of this cell so Tyler could pick one with him.

"Not at all. My date was boring." Carter unbuttoned his blazer and loosened his tie. "I can assume you didn't assault the man in question?"

"I did not."

"And the boy?"

"Miguel."

"Right. You know where he is?"

"Community services," he said, and handed him Nora Sullivan's number. Miguel and Louisa should be with Juliette by now, and therefore safe. That was all that mattered.

He tried to convince himself that his heart didn't matter. The cold stone stare in Juliette's eyes didn't matter. The future stretching out grim and wasted—none of it mattered.

If Miguel and Louisa could be with Juliette, then part of the night was a success.

"What happened here, Tyler?"

"The kid is a friend—"

"Not your usual kind."

Tyler thought of the attempted car theft and the extortion, the way Miguel had lied to get Richard to teach him cards. "He's exactly the usual kind. He's just sixteen and he was protecting his sister."

"It was self-defense?" Carter asked, taking the card. "And there's proof?"

"The little girl's face is about all the proof you need. Nora will answer all your questions."

Carter tilted his head, his icy-blue eyes watching him carefully. "You okay?"

Okay? He was so far from okay he was in a different time zone. A different hemisphere.

"Sure," he said, sitting on the bench in his cell.

"You know, Ty," Carter said, wrapping his hand around one of the bars. "You may have the rest of the world fooled, but I'm your brother."

It was about as close to a speech of brotherly love as Carter ever got.

"Get me out of here, Carter," he whispered.

"Right," Carter said, and then left to go show a cop he didn't know his butt from a hole in the ground.

Tyler dropped his head back against the wall so hard he saw stars. The pain was cleansing. Real. Gave all his rage something to do.

I was a fool to think you'd changed.

Her words wrapped around his brain, squeezing until he couldn't think of anything else. Anything but the fact that he *had* changed—but too late for it to mean anything.

"There are no charges," Carter said, coming back into the cell. "We're free to go."

CHAPTER NINETEEN

"RICHARD DID QUITE A NUMBER on Margot's stock," Carter said, reaching into the back of the liquor cabinet for a dusty bottle of Scotch.

"I'll replace it," Tyler said, staring out the kitchen window at the dark back courtyard. The moon hung low in the sky like a giant grapefruit.

"You don't have to keep cleaning up that guy's mess," Carter muttered.

"Dad being found with the gem is going to cause problems for you, isn't it?" Tyler asked.

Carter's face was dark. "You have no idea."

The glass of the greenhouse gleamed silver in places, obsidian in others, and it was so beautiful, suddenly there was nowhere Tyler would rather be than in Margot's greenhouse.

He opened the back door and crossed the dark courtyard. The grass under his feet, the air around him—everything seemed more alive than he felt.

I'm empty, he thought. *Half-dead.*

The greenhouse door opened with a slight push and inside the smell of earth and flowers was somehow both comforting and suffocating.

I could go, he thought. It's what people expected of him. Savannah. Juliette, hell, probably even Priscilla.

He turned on the hose, trickling water into the hanging pots that were beginning to sprout.

Carter stood in the doorway, the moon spreading his long shadow across Tyler's face and over his hands.

"You've been taking care of them?" he asked, handing Tyler a jam-jar glass of Scotch and taking a sip from his own.

"Someone needed to."

"You always did spend a lot of time in here when you were a kid."

"It was quiet," he said.

Carter laughed. "You gonna pretend you weren't hiding those dirty magazines behind the bags of soil?"

"Nope." Tyler smiled as he took a sip from his jam glass. "Not going to pretend."

The silence between them soon turned uncomfortable and it raked over his already raw emotions.

Carter was right—they were brothers, and that should count for something. But they stood here little better than strangers.

"How come you haven't been back?" Tyler asked, drinking half his Scotch down in one go. The urge to fight was still bubbling through him.

"I was back a month ago."

"For what? A few hours?"

"You're hardly one to talk, Tyler."

"I had Dad on me like a leech, Carter. You think I'm about to bring him back here?" That was only part of the reason. The least of his many. And frankly, the only noble one. "We agreed that we'd try to protect Savannah."

"Didn't matter, did it? He still found his way in."

"Yeah, well, he should be out of the picture for good now."

Carter chuckled, staring down at his Scotch as if it was tea leaves divining his fortune. "Don't be so sure," he said. "If I had a nickel for every time I thought that about Mom…"

"You've been in touch with her?" he asked, stunned. Angry. "And you didn't bother to tell me?"

"It was my business, Tyler." Carter's jaw was made out of stone and it made Tyler want to break it. "Not yours."

"Ah, the O'Neill family motto. It's no wonder we haven't all been together in years."

"That's not my fault," Carter said, putting his glass down with a thunk as if he was ready to throw a punch.

Finally, Tyler thought with glee, cranking off the hose and tossing his own glass down on the table. The fight he'd been waiting for. He'd hate to bust up Margot's greenhouse, but some things just couldn't be helped.

"You know what else isn't my fault?" Carter asked. "You screwing it up with Juliette, again. That's what you're really mad about. You don't care about me or the family, you're just pissed that you couldn't keep your shit together and now she's gone. Again."

It was a wild low blow. Terrible. It made him regret even mentioning her name on the way back to The Manor, but the truth of what Carter said rippled through him like a shock wave.

There was nothing for him to do but laugh. It was laugh or scream.

The sound crawled up from his gut, scraped through his throat.

"What's so funny?" Carter asked, advancing around the center table, his eyes alight.

"I feel bad for you, Carter. I do."

"Really? You feel bad for me? The man who left a third date that was no doubt going to end in sex to drive you home from jail? *Again?*"

"You should get arrested once, Carter. It would do you

good. Make you stop caring so goddamned much what people think of you. What are you hiding behind that perfect coat, that perfect hair?"

The punch came out of nowhere, catching him right across the jaw and snapping his head back.

Tyler charged Carter, grabbing him by the shirt and pushing him out the door into the night. They tripped and Carter spilled backward, Tyler following and landing hard on his brother.

"It's hard being an O'Neill, isn't it?" Tyler asked, pressing Carter's face into the dirt. "But it's gotta be harder pretending you're not one."

Carter got a knee up under Tyler's ribcage and he rolled backward. Carter might look prissy, but the guy was strong. Luckily, Tyler fought dirty, but soon it didn't matter.

There was so much Tyler was fighting against. Juliette. Jasper. His own stupid decision making. His brother. Every year he'd spent away from his sister. It all coalesced and imploded. His rage ate itself until suddenly there was nothing left to fight.

It was just him and every mistake he'd ever made.

The anger bottomed out. He let go of Carter and he flopped backward onto the grass. Carter did the same, breathing hard, his pristine shirt stained with blood and grass.

That made Tyler a little happy.

"We should have come back more," Carter panted. "For Savannah."

"I'm staying," Tyler said between breaths. Despite what had happened with Juliette, despite and maybe because of what everyone expected of him, Tyler was going to stick around.

Finally be the man he wanted to be.

"For how long?" Carter asked, and immediately put up his hand. "It's just a question. Don't get pissy."

"I'm not putting a limit on it, Carter. I want a home and this one feels good."

"It's not for Juliette, is it?"

Tyler shook his head, staring up at the stars while his lip started to swell. "I ruined it."

Carter smiled. "She kept you in that jail cell for hours with no charges. That is one pissed off woman, but I understand love can make fools of women. She may decide you're not so bad after all."

"There are only so many times a man can break a woman's heart before she gets wise."

Saying the words made the pain more bleak, cemented what he knew to be true. It didn't matter whether he stayed—Juliette was done with him.

So staying was for him. All for him. And it was still the right call.

At least he had that, a small island to cling to.

"Mom's going to come back, you know," Carter said, and there was something in his tone that made Tyler turn to look at him. Something resigned. And scared. "Now that the diamond has been found, she won't give up until she gets the ruby."

"It's not here," Tyler said, wondering what was between Carter and their mother. "We looked. We looked everywhere. The diamond was in literally the last place we searched."

"Mom knows where it is."

"How?"

"From what I've been able to put together, Mom dropped them here after the original heist and I think Margot found them."

"You having Mom followed or something?"

"It's my business, Tyler."

"Fine, Carter. But if Margot had a fortune in gems, why in the world is this house falling down? Why hasn't she—"

"Everyone has secrets, Tyler. Everyone."

"I don't," Tyler said, lying back down on the cold grass, staring up at the cold stars. "Not anymore."

JULIETTE PUSHED OPEN the door to her spare bedroom. In the three days since the kids had moved in, she'd been working like a demon. She'd gotten rid of the old double bed and bookshelves and replaced them with two single beds and some dressers. She'd let Miguel and Louisa pick out decorations and now one half of the room was covered in basketball posters while the other half was a shrine to Hannah Montana.

But tonight, as it had been for the past three, the bed with the pink sheets was empty.

Louisa lay next to her brother, the two of them sleeping back to back, their knees pulled to their chests. Like twins in vitro.

They'd spent a week in a small group home while Juliette's foster-parent application was approved, and the counselor there said Miguel and Louisa had slept that way every night.

She pulled the door shut and pressed her forehead against the frame until the wood bit into her scalp.

There was a war going on inside of her. A constant battle between joy and grief.

The kids were here and they were safe. And against all odds, they seemed to be doing okay with the transition. Miguel was apologetic all the time, and Louisa was slowly returning to her old self, as long as Miguel was around.

She'd taken the week off to help the kids adjust. She had some adjusting to do herself.

Her father had turned into a surprise ally. He'd helped her put together the furniture, and last night he'd cooked chili and then stuck around to play Rummikub with the kids.

It had been one of the more surreal moments of her life.

They didn't talk about Tyler. They didn't talk about much, to be honest, but the quiet between them was comfortable.

It was as close to peaceful as she got these days, since she was fighting off a constant urge to call Tyler. To see him. To handcuff him to something and strip away every single layer of the man until there was nothing but the truth of him left. If there was any.

It was a bloody fight, and she didn't know how much longer she could hold out.

She walked away from the kids' room and into her dark living room. A family picture on her mantel caught the light from her kitchen and her parents' faces, before Mom's cancer, smiled up at her.

You really don't understand how someone can be torn in their loyalties? she asked herself.

She tried to forget Tyler's face as she'd left him in that cell, walking away with her father. It must have killed him.

"Juliette?" Miguel whispered from behind her. "You okay?"

"I'm fine," she said, turning with a smile for the boy. "What are you doing up?"

Miguel wrapped the bottom of his T-shirt around his arm, a nervous habit of his she'd noticed. "I want to go to work for Tyler after school."

"Has he talked to you?" she asked, far too eagerly.

"No, but I was supposed to start last Monday and…well, I didn't."

"Right." She licked her lips. "You want to go out to the build site tomorrow?"

He nodded. "I sort of promised, you know?"

She wanted to hug him, to pull the boy to her and tell him how proud she was of him. Of how, from the moment she'd met him, defiant and pissed, being brought into the station in handcuffs from that fight with his father in the grocery store, she'd felt that he would change her life.

And that she'd hoped she could change his.

"Okay then," she said, knowing it was too soon, that her relationship with Miguel was fragile and too much pressure might destroy it somehow. "We'll go see Tyler tomorrow."

"SHE'S SLEEPING SO MUCH," Miguel said the next day after school as they bounced their way down the gravel road toward the build site.

Juliette glanced in the rearview mirror at Louisa, slouched and snoring in the backseat.

"Is that normal?" Miguel asked.

Juliette smiled, her heart twisting in her chest. "I imagine she's got a lot of catching up to do," she said. "I doubt she's slept well in a long time. It's kind of like you and eating." She glanced sideways at the boy, who was systematically eating her out of house and home. She needed to keep up the chatter. The distraction. Because she was driving out to see Tyler. To talk to him.

It felt as though her body might explode from her seething, battling emotions. From her worry that the second she saw him she'd collapse into tears, begging him to tell her why he'd lied. Begging him to take her back.

But it would be a mistake. She knew that. He hadn't changed; he might not be able to. Tyler O'Neill might just be the best bad boy out there. A heart full of good intentions, but a nature more prone to destruction.

She hated to think it. Didn't want to believe it. But it had been proven time and time again.

"Juliette?" Miguel asked. "When do we go back to my dad?"

Juliette whirled to face him. "What? Why? Do you want to go back? Do you not like it at my house?"

"No," Miguel assured her quickly. "We love it there, but I figure we need to get ready for going back."

Juliette pulled over to the side of the road, unaware that Miguel was so misinformed about his circumstances. "Your dad is in jail," she told him. "Until the trial. And after that, I imagine the court will rule to take you two away from him."

"So, what happens when I'm eighteen?" he asked with a careful smile that set her body buzzing.

"You can appeal to be made guardian of your sister or…" She stopped. She hadn't really thought about this, and putting words to these very thin and delicate ideas seemed foolish. Too early.

"What?"

"Well, after the trial you'll be a ward of the state, and as long as you like it there, and I like you there, and we keep passing the home inspections, you can stay at my house."

"That's good." Miguel seemed to be reading her hesitation the wrong way. "Isn't it?"

"It is, Miguel. It's really good. I'm so happy you guys are in my house. But what are you going to do when you're eighteen?"

"I'll get a job or something, I guess. An apartment for me and Louisa?"

"What about college or learning some kind of trade? You can't do that and take care of your sister at the same time. And what if one of you gets sick? You should have help, Miguel. Eighteen might seem like a grown-up, but you're still a kid. And you should get to have the chance to be a kid."

Miguel shook his head at her, his face blank. "I'm not following, Chief."

"I could adopt you," she blurted, and squeezed her eyes shut. "I could adopt you both."

The quiet in the car was long and deep and finally she looked over at him. He stared at her, mouth hanging open, eyes wide.

"You kidding?" he asked.

She shook her head.

"You saying this 'cause you feel bad for me? You think I can't take care of Louisa?"

He was so defensive, ready to fight the world for his sister, and she just couldn't admire the kid more. "I think you can take care of you sister just fine. I just want someone…" She paused. "I want to take care of you, Miguel."

Miguel turned to stare out the window and she didn't know what he was thinking. If this was good. Or bad. If he was insulted.

"Think about it, okay?" she finally said, wondering if she'd just made a huge mistake. "Just think about it."

He nodded but didn't say anything, and after a moment she started the car again and continued to drive out to the build site.

Surveyors were putting up flags, marking the areas where the individual houses would be built, and men were climbing into little Bobcats and diggers, getting ready to level the land for the concrete pour.

It was busy. Really busy. And in the middle of it all was Tyler. An unforeseen conductor. A surprise leader.

The second she drove up, Tyler—wearing a hard hat and those perfect jeans that made her body sweat—turned away from the men he'd been talking to and approached the car.

Her heart thundered in her chest.

"Hey, Tyler!" Miguel said, hurtling out of the car before she even had it in Park. "Sorry I wasn't here on Monday—"

"It's okay," Tyler said, clapping Miguel on the shoulder. Juliette could see the emotion in Tyler's eyes, the relief and the love he felt for that boy. She had to look away, his visible emotions tearing at her walls, her carefully crafted distance.

"I'm glad you're here today," Tyler said to Miguel. "You ready to work?"

Miguel nodded.

"Attaboy. Go see Derek over there and he'll get you set up."

Miguel was off like a shot. Tyler watched him go and then slowly, turned to face Juliette.

CHAPTER TWENTY

HER BODY FLOODED WITH HEAT, icy hot prickles of awareness that stung her flesh. She clenched and unclenched her hands, smoothed down the front of her shirt.

As his long slow stride brought him over to the car, she found herself breathless. Waiting.

He ducked, smiling when he saw Louisa in the backseat.

"It worked. They're with you now," he said, clearly relieved, and she knew she should have called him earlier. To thank him. To tell him that everyone was safe. But she'd been a coward for two weeks, scared of what other things she might have said. What might have tumbled out of her mouth.

She got out of the car. "I should have called—"

He waved her off. "You don't owe me anything," he said. "I'm just glad it worked out. Everyone's doing all right?"

She nodded, words completely beyond her.

"Good," he said. "That's…good."

They both looked out at the work and Juliette was stunned to see her father out there holding one of the surveyor flags.

"Is that my dad?" she asked.

"I couldn't believe it, either," Tyler said, "but a few days ago he came out here saying he wanted to work."

"With you?"

"He doesn't talk to me, but every once in a while he'll

nod. Yesterday he told me to have a good night." Tyler shrugged. "He didn't tell you?"

Juliette reeled. Her father? And Tyler? She felt the need to check the sky for flying swine.

"No," she said. "He didn't."

If he can do it, a small voice whispered in the back of her head. *So can you.*

"You're still staying?" she asked.

"Lots of work to do."

She glanced up at Tyler only to find him watching her. His smile was the saddest thing she'd ever seen. Hopeless. Lost. And she wanted to have a hard heart, she wanted to be unaffected, but it was impossible. Part of Tyler O'Neill lived under her skin and she would never be impervious.

The truth was, she understood why he lied. How in his head it was all right. He was protecting the people he loved in the only way he knew how. With secrets and deceit and self-sacrifice.

It was wrong, but everything he did, he did because he loved her, the knowledge seeping through the bedrock of her anger.

A light went on in her head. Her heart.

Tyler O'Neill just needed to be shown a different way to love.

He wasn't that different from Miguel—scared of the unknown and making decisions out of fear. Betrayed by people who should love him.

The battle in her turned and sharpened and now she was fighting for him. For him to see her, really see her, and understand that she stood in front of him a whole person.

"I don't need protecting," she said, and his eyes, electric in their intensity, swung to her.

"You're the toughest, strongest woman I know, Juliette. I was stupid to think you needed me to protect you."

"And I don't need you making decisions for me."

He nodded. "I won't make that mistake again."

"You told me you wanted to show me the best of yourself," she said.

"I did," he said. "I do."

"I want to do the same," she said, feeling as though she was in midair, suspended between trust and doubt. Between her wants and her fears.

She thought of her father, alone in that big house that used to know love. Doubt and mistrust had been Jasper's roommates, his only friends.

That could be her one day. She knew it. A few years from now, and she could still hold this grudge against Tyler. She could still see only the hurt he'd caused her and never pay any attention to why.

But Jasper had found his way out of that house.

And Tyler was the key.

If there was one thing Miguel had shown her, it was that context was everything. Circumstances mattered. And Tyler's context was complicated.

There was a light in Tyler, dim right now, but growing brighter every moment. It was Tyler as he should be.

Noble and good. Human, but trying to rise above the worst of himself.

I can do that, too, she thought, inspired by his beauty, his courage and his effort. *I want to do that.*

"I want to show you the best of myself, too, but I don't know what that is," she said, the truth actually hard to say. "All I've done is doubt you—"

"For good reason, Juliette. Christ, I've hurt you and lied—"

"You keep absolving me of guilt," she said, "like I've had

no part in what's happened to us. Like I've done nothing wrong, and that's not true. Priscilla told me that I wanted to believe the best in you but couldn't get past the worst, and she's right. The second things went south, I doubted you. And I *was* interrogating you that day at The Manor. And maybe you lied because I never really showed you how much I trusted you."

His eyes went wide. "I don't blame you, Juliette."

"Tyler." She couldn't help but smile, and once she did, tears bit hard into her eyes. Love filled her heart. "I know you don't. But maybe you should blame me a little more and yourself a little less."

She reached out for his hand, lacing her fingers through his. Pressing her palm to his, she felt every callus. Every heartbeat.

He clutched at her hand, his strength taking her breath away. "Let's go slow," she whispered. "Take our time."

"Where are we going?" he asked, pulling her in closer, winding the fingers of his other hand through hers, until they stood there, smiling at each other, holding hands as if the world might tear them apart any moment.

"Anywhere," she whispered. "I'll go anywhere as long as I'm with you."

EPILOGUE

One Month Later

IT WAS THE END OF THE NIGHT and Juliette could not contain any more joy. She was full—her hands, her heart, her whole damn body—full of as much happiness as she could hold.

Margot, Savannah and Matt were home and the party had been grand—even Carter had come home for it.

But still, she looked in the shadows under the grand cypress in the back courtyard for Tyler.

Because no amount of happiness was enough if Tyler wasn't there.

She found him, sprawled in a chair, his shirt half-unbuttoned.

"Hey, baby," he said, his voice liquid like his hand on her back, fingers down her spine, and she smiled. "Where are the kids?"

"Margot let them have the sleeping porch. They're out cold."

He held out his hand to pull her into his lap and she went willingly, though she rearranged herself to straddle his thighs.

"Well, well," he said, his half smile the sexiest thing she'd ever seen. He wrapped his arms around her hips and pulled her closer.

Juliette lay into him, her face in his neck breathing in the warm spice that was Tyler.

"Miguel told me he wants to go on with the emancipation paperwork," she said. The trial had been last week and Ramon was going to jail. Emancipation was the first step toward adoption.

"What?" he asked, pushing her away slightly so he could look into her eyes. "Really?"

She nodded.

"That is good news," he whispered, his voice gruff.

In that moment she made her decision. Or rather, she pushed her mind out of the equation and let her heart lead the way.

A month ago, she would never have expected to do this. But over the past three weeks, she'd come to realize just what kind of man Tyler was.

The best kind of man.

"I love you," she said. "Have I told you that?"

"Not enough," he said, pressing a kiss to her shoulder. "Have I told you you have a great butt?"

She laughed, she kept laughing until she couldn't stop the tears.

"Hey," he said, lifting her up so he could see her face, wipe away her tears. "Come on now, what's this?"

"I'm happy, Tyler," she said. "I'm so happy."

"That's great, Jules. Me, too."

"I've changed my mind," she said.

"About what?" he asked.

She licked her lips, thinking she needed to gather her courage, her belief and trust. But it was simply right there. Everything she felt for Tyler was so much a part of the happiness she felt, and she knew that this moment, all the moments ahead with Miguel and Louisa, were only possible because of him.

"I don't want to go slow," she said. "Not anymore."

"We can go faster," he said, his hands sliding up over her hips.

"Tyler." She put her hands on his, stopping him.

His eyes met hers and it took a moment, but he clued in and his slow smile revealed the future.

And it was perfect.

"I don't want to adopt those children without you," she said. "I can't imagine being a family if you're not in it."

His head snapped back as if she'd slapped him and then tears welled up in his eyes.

"Are you sure?" he whispered, his face twisted between doubt and joy and she clapped her hands to his face.

"I couldn't be more sure of anything in my life," she said emphatically.

"Marry me," he said.

"I thought you'd never ask."

* * * * *

Don't miss the exciting conclusion to
THE NOTORIOUS O'NEILLS.
Look for
THE SCANDAL AND CARTER O'NEILL
by Molly O'Keefe
in October 2010 from Harlequin Superromance.

HARLEQUIN® *Super Romance*®

COMING NEXT MONTH

Available October 12, 2010

#1662 THE GOOD PROVIDER
Spotlight on Sentinel Pass
Debra Salonen

#1663 THE SCANDAL AND CARTER O'NEILL
The Notorious O'Neills
Molly O'Keefe

#1664 ADOPTED PARENTS
Suddenly a Parent
Candy Halliday

#1665 CALLING THE SHOTS
You, Me & the Kids
Ellen Hartman

#1666 THAT RUNAWAY SUMMER
Return to Indigo Springs
Darlene Gardner

#1667 DANCE WITH THE DOCTOR
Single Father
Cindi Myers

LARGER-PRINT BOOKS!
GET 2 FREE LARGER-PRINT NOVELS PLUS
2 FREE GIFTS!

HARLEQUIN®

Super Romance®

Exciting, emotional, unexpected!

YES! Please send me 2 FREE LARGER-PRINT Harlequin® Superromance® novels and my 2 FREE gifts (gifts are worth about $10). After receiving them, if I don't wish to receive any more books, I can return the shipping statement marked "cancel." If I don't cancel, I will receive 6 brand-new novels every month and be billed just $5.44 per book in the U.S. or $5.99 per book in Canada. That's a saving of at least 13% off the cover price! It's quite a bargain! Shipping and handling is just 50¢ per book.* I understand that accepting the 2 free books and gifts places me under no obligation to buy anything. I can always return a shipment and cancel at any time. Even if I never buy another book from Harlequin, the two free books and gifts are mine to keep forever.

139/339 HDN E5PS

Name _____ (PLEASE PRINT) _____

Address _____ Apt. # _____

City _____ State/Prov. _____ Zip/Postal Code _____

Signature (if under 18, a parent or guardian must sign) _____

Mail to the **Harlequin Reader Service:**
IN U.S.A.: P.O. Box 1867, Buffalo, NY 14240-1867
IN CANADA: P.O. Box 609, Fort Erie, Ontario L2A 5X3

Not valid for current subscribers to Harlequin Superromance Larger-Print books.

**Are you a current subscriber to Harlequin Superromance books
and want to receive the larger-print edition?
Call 1-800-873-8635 today!**

* Terms and prices subject to change without notice. Prices do not include applicable taxes. N.Y. residents add applicable sales tax. Canadian residents will be charged applicable provincial taxes and GST. Offer not valid in Quebec. This offer is limited to one order per household. All orders subject to approval. Credit or debit balances in a customer's account(s) may be offset by any other outstanding balance owed by or to the customer. Please allow 4 to 6 weeks for delivery. Offer available while quantities last.

Your Privacy: Harlequin Books is committed to protecting your privacy. Our Privacy Policy is available online at www.eHarlequin.com or upon request from the Reader Service. From time to time we make our lists of customers available to reputable third parties who may have a product or service of interest to you. If you would prefer we not share your name and address, please check here. ☐

Help us get it right—We strive for accurate, respectful and relevant communications. To clarify or modify your communication preferences, visit us at www.ReaderService.com/consumerschoice.

HSRLP10R

HARLEQUIN®

A Romance

FOR EVERY MOOD™

Spotlight on

Inspirational

Wholesome romances
that touch the heart and soul.

See the next page
to enjoy a sneak peek from
the Love Inspired® inspirational series.

CATINSPLI10

*See below for a sneak peek at
our inspirational line, Love Inspired®.
Introducing HIS HOLIDAY BRIDE
by bestselling author Jillian Hart*

Autumn Granger gave her horse rein to slide toward the town's new sheriff.

"Hey, there." The man in a brand-new Stetson, black T-shirt, jeans and riding boots held up a hand in greeting. He stepped away from his four-wheel drive with "Sheriff" in black on the doors and waded through the grasses. "I'm new around here."

"I'm Autumn Granger."

"Nice to meet you, Miss Granger. I'm Ford Sherman, from Chicago." He knuckled back his hat, revealing the most handsome face she'd ever seen. Big blue eyes contrasted with his sun-tanned complexion.

"I'm guessing you haven't seen much open land. Out here, you've got to keep an eye on cows or they're going to tear your vehicle apart."

"What?" He whipped around. Sure enough, mammoth black-and-white creatures had started to gnaw on his four-wheel drive. They clustered like a mob, mouths and tongues and teeth bent on destruction. One cow tried to pry the wiper off the windshield, another chewed on the side mirror. Several leaned through the open window, licking the seats.

"Move along, little dogie." He didn't know the first thing about cattle.

The entire herd swiveled their heads to study him curiously. Not a single hoof shifted. The animals soon returned to chewing, licking, digging through his possessions.

Autumn laughed, a warm and wonderful sound. "Thanks,

I needed that." She then pulled a bag from behind her saddle and waved it at the cows. "Look what I have, guys. Cookies."

Cows swung in her direction, and dozens of liquid brown eyes brightened with cookie hopes. As she circled the car, the cattle bounded after her. The earth shook with the force of their powerful hooves.

"Next time, you're on your own, city boy." She tipped her hat. The cowgirl stayed on his mind, the sweetest thing he had ever seen.

Will Ford be able to stick it out in the country
to find out more about Autumn?
Find out in HIS HOLIDAY BRIDE
by bestselling author Jillian Hart,
available in October 2010
only from Love Inspired®.